Dear Reader,

The inspiration for this book came from an unusual source—my sister. We had both just watched *The Thomas Crown Affair* (the one with Pierce Brosnan) and she was complaining that the story was supposed to be her life, not the heroine's! She was certain some quirk of fate had deprived her of a life that included a private jet, an international playboy and scads of designer clothes.

I think being swept away by a wealthy playboy might be a pretty popular fantasy, one I decided to explore in *Into the Night*. After finishing the book, I'd have to say that, given the same offer—a quick getaway to a beautiful island—I wouldn't hesitate to hop onto a plane with a sexy stranger, either!

I hope you enjoy this Forbidden Fantasy. For those of you wondering about the Quinns—there will be more coming later this year! Stay tuned.

Happy New Year!

Kate Hoffmann

Kate Hoffmann

INTO THE NIGHT

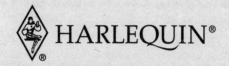

HARLEQUIN®

TORONTO • NEW YORK • LONDON
AMSTERDAM • PARIS • SYDNEY • HAMBURG
STOCKHOLM • ATHENS • TOKYO • MILAN • MADRID
PRAGUE • WARSAW • BUDAPEST • AUCKLAND

Recycling programs
for this product may
not exist in your area.

ISBN-13: 978-0-373-79589-5

INTO THE NIGHT

Copyright © 2011 by Peggy A. Hoffmann

ABOUT THE AUTHOR

Kate Hoffmann began writing for Harlequin Books in 1993. Since then she's published sixty books, primarily in the Harlequin Temptation and Harlequin Blaze lines. When she isn't writing, she enjoys music, theater and musical theater. She is active, working with high school students in the performing arts. She lives in southeastern Wisconsin with her two cats, Chloe and Tally.

Books by Kate Hoffmann

Don't miss any of our special offers. Write to us at the following address for information on our newest releases.

Harlequin Reader Service
U.S.: 3010 Walden Ave., P.O. Box 1325, Buffalo, NY 14269
Canadian: P.O. Box 609, Fort Erie, Ont. L2A 5X3

1

T<small>ESS</small> R<small>OBERTSON</small> <small>STEPPED</small> through the doors of the Perryman Hotel, nodding at the doorman as she passed. The lobby of Nashville's most luxurious hotel was decorated for the Christmas holidays, although the atmosphere was now buzzing with the excitement of the upcoming New Year's weekend.

She searched the scattered guests, lounging on upholstered sofas and chairs. A few of them glanced over at her and she wondered if they could see right through her elegant facade. Maybe that saying was true. You can take a girl out of the country, but you can never take the country out of the girl.

Her gaze dropped to her shoes, purchased just that morning, along with her dress and the small clutch purse she had gripped in her hand. The sexy shoes pinched and the sleek bag barely held more than money, a lipstick and her cell phone. But she had to admit the dress was the prettiest thing she'd ever owned, worth every penny she'd charged on her credit card. It was important she looked her best tonight. For the first time in the five years she'd worked for the Beale family, she'd been invited to their annual New Year's Eve party.

The Beales, Frank and Nan, and their son, Jeffrey, were Tennessee gentry, their old family money made in industry—cotton, tobacco and shipping—and now invested in commercial real estate and the thoroughbred farm she managed for them outside Lexington, Kentucky. They wintered in Palm Beach and summered at a mountain estate near Asheville, leaving their vast business concerns to Jeffrey, their thirty-three-year-old only son.

Though people like the Beales moved in a very different world from Tess's, their paths often intersected at the farm and at all the important horse races—the Derby, the Preakness, Belmont. Still, there had always been an invisible wall between them—the Beales relaxed in a luxury box while she worked in the stables. They wore beautiful clothes and she dressed in jeans. They traveled on private jets and she rode in a pickup truck, pulling a horse trailer. The rich were very different—except for Jeffrey.

"Tess!"

She spun around to find her best friend, Alison Cole, hurrying across the lobby, her heels clicking on the marble floor as she walked.

"Sorry I'm late," Alison said. "Have you been here long?" She leaned close and hugged Tess. "How was your Christmas? And your Dad? Good I hope." She stepped back and gave Tess a quick perusal. "You look fabulous! You clean up very well." She examined Tess's hair and nodded in approval. "No hay. That's a good sign."

Tess's spirits brightened. "Do you really like the dress? It was between this and a blue one. The blue one made my chest look enormous, but I thought this garnet color was more sophisticated."

They both glanced around the lobby, realizing that Tess had spoken a little too loudly. "Good choice," Alison said with a laugh.

"Well, it's true," Tess whispered, silently reminding herself to think before she spoke. It was one of her worst habits, one she was trying to change.

"Now, tell me, why was it so important that I come along with you to this party? You hang around these people all the time. Why are you nervous about tonight?"

Tess grabbed Alison's hand and led her toward the bar. "I'll explain everything over a drink. I don't want to get upstairs too early. I haven't eaten all day and the buffet will be too much to resist. You know I have absolutely no willpower when it comes to crab claws."

Once they'd settled themselves at the bar, Tess took a gulp of her vodka tonic, then drew a deep breath. "I think Jeffrey is going to propose to me tonight," she said, the words tumbling out of her mouth.

Alison gasped, her eyes going wide. "What?"

"I've been expecting it for a while. We've been carrying on this relationship for about four years and I can tell he's getting…restless. When he was at the farm a couple weeks ago, he told me he was going to make a very important announcement at the party tonight and that I might be surprised. Then, out of nowhere, I get an invitation. I've never been invited before. And this would be so him, shocking his parents with the news that he wants to marry me. I can just see him, getting down on his knee at midnight in front of all these people."

"Have you even discussed marriage?"

"No, not really," Tess said. "But it makes perfect sense for both of us. We make a good team."

"And you love him?"

Tess hesitated before answering. It was a question she'd asked herself over and over again. The answer seemed to change like the weather. "He can give me the security I never had, and I can be a good wife to him." She shook her head. "I know you've never really liked him, but—"

"No," Alison said. "It's not that I don't like him. I don't know him. We've never met. You're the only one who knows him. This whole relationship exists in the dark, Tess. No one has a clue anything's going on between you. Don't you find that strange?"

"We both wanted it that way," Tess insisted. "It would have caused too many problems if everyone at the farm thought I was sleeping with the boss. And you know my father. Give him a few drinks and he'd be bragging about it to all his buddies. Besides, the Beales have always wanted Jeffrey to marry someone from a prominent family. He's trying to protect me."

Alison shook her head, turning back to her drink. "I just think it's a little weird."

Tess reached out and touched her arm. "I know it is. But we're two very practical people. We respect each other. We're both focused on our work. And even though the sex isn't earth-shattering, it's enough for me. I can be very happy with that."

"I thought I could, too," Alison said. "But when you find the real thing, you'll feel much differently. Think about yourself for once, Tess. Don't worry about your father or your finances."

That was easy for Alison to say, Tess mused. Alison had two parents who had loved and cared for her and two sisters to support her along the way. All Tess had was an alcoholic father who'd drifted from job to job during her childhood and gambled away any chance they ever had at a stable home life.

Tess had become *his* caretaker at the age of seven, at the moment her mother had walked out nearly twenty years ago. How many times had they been homeless since that day? How many days had they scraped out a living doing menial labor on horse farms just to eat? She knew exactly what Jeffrey's money would buy. Tess would finally have a home of her own, a place in the world that wasn't dependant on keeping her job.

"I know what I'm doing," Tess said.

"Then why am I here? Are you sure you didn't want me to talk you out of this?"

"Moral support. I need at least one person in that

room on my side. And I can say anything to you. You understand me."

"You should be able to say anything to Jeffrey, too," Alison said. "You shouldn't have to pretend to be something you're not, Tess."

"I'm not pretending," Tess countered. "I'm just moderating my bad habits." She straightened. "He lives in a whole different world, with different rules. I just want to fit in."

Up until the time she'd entered college, Tess and her father had been gypsies, outsiders who never stayed in one place more than a year. From upstate New York to Florida to California, back and forth across the country, Tess had made friends only to lose them.

She'd met Alison their freshman year in college at University of Kentucky in Lexington. They were both there on scholarship and spent long nights working at various campus jobs to make ends meet. Alison was Tess's first and only true friend.

"Do you really think I'm settling?" Tess asked.

"I just want you to be happy. You deserve a guy who makes your heart race, one who can't live without you. A guy who loves you exactly the way you are." She paused. "How do *you* feel? Can you live without him?"

"Of course I can," Tess said. She stopped short, realizing she'd spoken too quickly. It wasn't the answer Ali wanted to hear. "You know what I mean. I've been providing for us since I could muck out a stall. I just meant that it's possible—to live without him. To live without anybody." She paused, her voice going soft. "I know what I want." Tess took a long gulp of her drink then set the glass in front of her.

"You also deserve a man who doesn't want to keep your relationship a secret," Alison continued. "Who doesn't have to explain his feelings for you to his parents—who doesn't send you an engraved invitation to show up for his marriage proposal."

"Stop!" Tess cried. "Have *you* found this paragon of manhood? I don't know if he exists. I could wait my entire life and never find him." She looked over at Alison to find a tiny smile twitching at the corners of her friend's mouth. "What? You have?"

"I'm almost afraid to talk about it," Alison said. "It's so new. But it is *so* incredible. We just can't seem to keep our hands off each other. He's a doctor. And he works out of a little clinic in the mountains, a few hours from Johnson City. I've only known him about a month, but it's like we've been together forever. He's sweet and sexy and funny and he's turned my life upside down. And I love him."

"Then why aren't you with him tonight?"

"Because you said you needed me here. And you're my dearest friend." Alison smiled coyly. "All right. He's upstairs, naked, in bed, enjoying treats from the mini-bar and watching a hockey game until I get back. I'm planning to rejoin him as soon as my duties as best friend are completed."

"Oh, no you don't!" Tess cried. "You don't need to stay with me. I'm just being silly. Go back to your naked man."

"He's just fine," Alison said.

"Really. I can do this on my own," Tess insisted. "And after Jeffrey proposes, I'll bring him downstairs and introduce you. Then I can meet your doctor."

"Or maybe we can get together for breakfast tomorrow?" Alison suggested. "Or brunch?"

"All right," Tess agreed, anxious to send Alison on her way. "Brunch."

"Are you ready?" Alison asked.

She shook her head. "No. I'm going finish my drink. Then I'll be ready. You go ahead. I'll talk to you later."

"All right. I'll see you tomorrow." Alison gave her a hug, then picked up her purse. "Listen to your heart, sweetie, and you'll be just fine." As Alison headed back out to the lobby, Tess grabbed a bowl of pretzels and munched on one, thinking about the way the evening might unfold.

She'd met Jeffrey when he'd visited the farm with his parents right after Derby Week four and a half years ago. She'd been working as the assistant manager at Beresford and Tess had thought he was handsome and friendly. There hadn't been an attraction, at least not on her part. But after he'd returned every weekend for a month with the excuse that he wanted to learn how to ride, they'd just fallen into a sexual relationship. Two years later, she was promoted from assistant manager to manager, due in part to Jeffrey's recommendation.

Though they secretly slept together whenever he was at the farm, they'd maintained a cordial business relationship outside the bedroom. Jeffrey had helped her learn how the stable fit into the Beale holdings and she'd taught him nearly everything she knew about the horse business.

Beyond their shared interests on the farm, they were quite compatible in the bedroom. Sex was enjoyable, if not a bit mundane. And Tess seemed to satisfy his needs. She'd never felt giddy or light-headed, never heard angels singing or saw fireworks when they were in bed together, but she'd written all that off as some silly schoolgirl myth.

The past few years, Jeffrey's family had been pressuring him to choose a wife and give them grandchildren. And though she and Jeffrey had discussed the subject of marriage—his marriage—their conversations had always just danced around her part in the equation. She knew he loved her. He'd told her that on a number of occasions. In her heart, she believed a marriage proposal was the next logical step.

So why did it feel as if she were settling? Perhaps, she was just too practical to lose herself in the pursuit of some fantasy man. In truth, she had a hard time imagining any relationship in which she could completely surrender her heart. The wounds of her childhood ran far too deep.

Tess studied her reflection in the mirror behind the bar. She'd taken special care with her appearance, knowing she'd want to look her best for the photos that would be taken. She'd chosen a dress of garnet Thai silk that shimmered with black and gold highlights as she moved.

A rhinestone necklace circled her neck, leaving the rest of her shoulders and chest bare.

Her attention was caught by the reflection of a man who had appeared at the other end of the bar. She studied his reflection silently, listening as he requested a bottle of scotch. He was the kind of gorgeous she didn't see very often, at least not working on a horse farm. Her stomach fluttered and she turned away, drawing a deep breath.

Tess ran her fingers through the soft curls of her shoulder-length hair, pushing the dark strands back into place. Though she wasn't a great beauty, she was pretty enough. Standing at Jeffrey's side, they made a handsome couple. If she set her mind to it, she could pass as someone who belonged in the Beales' social circle.

Tess took one last sip of her drink, then opened her purse and paid the bartender. But as she walked back through the lobby to the elevator, she began to doubt her resolve. Though she ought to be feeling exhilarated, all she could sense was a faint sense of dread. His parents wouldn't approve, the party guests wouldn't welcome her, and she be left as she always was—an outsider searching for a way in.

"So what else is new," she muttered, quickening her step. She'd been an outsider her entire life and had survived quite nicely. If Jeffrey asked, then she'd say yes. He was the only one who mattered. She didn't care what people thought.

Tess hurried toward the elevator. Though her nerves threatened to get the better of her, once she'd accepted his proposal she'd be fine. The doors to the elevator were just closing as she approached. "Hold the elevator!" she cried.

A hand appeared between the doors and they opened again. Tess hurried inside. "Thanks," she murmured as she punched the button for the top floor. There were plenty of marriages based on friendship, on respect, on mutual goals for the future. "It's not like I have men waiting in line," she murmured.

"What?"

She looked up and saw a familiar face. The man from the bar stood on the other side of the elevator, his piercing blue eyes suddenly stealing the breath from her lungs. She blinked, her ears suddenly filled with an odd ringing. "What?"

"You said something. I'm sorry, I thought you were talking to me."

"No. I was just thinking out loud." Her voice cracked. "Thanks. For holding the elevator."

"No problem."

They waited together for the doors to close, both of them staring back out into the lobby, Tess's heart slamming in her chest.

"Maybe you should push the button to close the door," he suggested.

She risked another glance over at him. Gawd, he was drop-dead sexy. She'd never seen a guy so beautiful. And it wasn't just the perfect features or the boyish smile or the thick, dark hair. He was dressed like he'd just stepped off the pages of a fashion magazine. From his suit to his immaculately tailored shirt to his silk tie, it was clear that there was a killer body beneath the clothes.

"The door?" he said.

"Yes," Tess murmured. "Thank you for holding it." Oh, God, she'd already said that.

He stepped around her, his shoulder brushing against hers as he passed, but then she realized what he wanted her to do. Stumbling forward, she reached for the button, but her legs were so wobbly, she tripped into the control panel.

A moment later, his fingers firmly closed around her elbow and he restored her balance. "Are you all right?"

"Yes," she said, busying herself by punching at the buttons for the door. "Fine." She pressed her hand to her chest and felt her heart pounding beneath her palm. This was how it was supposed to feel, Tess thought. This is what Alison had been talking about. Here she was, on her way to her own engagement party and she was flustered over a complete stranger.

"What floor did you want?" she asked.

"Twelve," he said. He pointed to the panel. "I pressed it when I got in."

"I'm going to the roof."

"Not planning to jump, are you?" he teased.

She gave him a sideways glance and found him smiling. "I'm considering it. But I'm afraid of heights."

"That would be fifteen, then," he replied, pointing to the panel.

She quickly reached out and punched the button again. Though Tess thought an outdoor party on the hotel's roof garden was a bit foolhardy in the middle of a Nashville winter, the Beales would no doubt bring in portable heaters to warm the chilly, damp air. Money was never an object with them. The roof of the Perryman was supposed to have a stunning view of the city and the river. Only the best for the Beales, regardless of the cost. Her engagement party would certainly be memorable.

He met her gaze again and she found herself staring into the most arresting eyes. There was a devilish twinkle in them that only intensified when he smiled. "It's going to be cold up there. Are you dressed warmly enough?"

She shrugged. "It's a party. I'm sure there will be tents and heaters." She nodded toward the bottle he held. "What about you? Are you going to a party too?"

He shook his head. "I'm not in a party mood. I plan to spend a quiet night in my room, maybe watch a movie."

"You and a bottle of scotch?" This time Tess met his gaze squarely, refusing to look away. "They say you should never drink alone."

"I know. It's such a cliché. But this is a very good bottle of scotch. And I haven't met anyone I'd be interested in sharing it with." He paused. "Until now."

She felt a warm blush creep up her cheeks and a shiver skittered down her spine. This was crazy. She was supposed to be in love with Jeffrey. Why was she even allowing herself to flirt with this stranger? Especially when she had absolutely no idea how to flirt.

"You look beautiful, by the way," he said, pointing the bottle in her direction. "That dress is…well, looking like that, you're going to be the prettiest girl at the party."

She hadn't imagined it. They were definitely flirting. And for the first time in her life, she felt as if she wasn't making a complete fool of herself. Tess had never really learned how to charm a man, how to draw him in and make him want her. She'd always blurted out something sarcastic or brutally honest, ruining the mood.

But this stranger seemed to be totally entranced by her. Tess felt her stomach drop as the elevator started moving up. She'd never put much thought into her appearance. But suddenly she was glad she had, if only to feel this way just once in her life. "Thank you. You're very…charming."

They were still smiling at each other when the elevator suddenly jerked. Tess fell back, slamming her shoulder against the wall. Crying out, she struggled to stay upright, but instead tumbled into his arms.

The lights in the car flickered and went out. Tess's breath caught in her throat as she waited, his body warm against hers, her breath coming in shallow gasps. This was it. This was God's punishment for flirting with a handsome stranger. She was about to plunge down to the basement and die on the very night she was supposed to get engaged. The Fates were cruel.

But when the elevator didn't drop, Tess wondered if

she wasn't being sent a different message. Maybe she wasn't supposed to go upstairs. Maybe this was exactly where she belonged.

DEREK NOLAN WAITED in the silence. His fingers gripped the woman's arms, her skin soft beneath his touch. She hadn't said anything since the lights went out and the elevator bumped to a stop. Though he couldn't see her, an image of her was still swimming around in his head.

Until she'd stepped into the elevator, he'd been having a rather unremarkable night. He'd been prepared to spend his evening alone, with room service and a glass of the hotel's best scotch, get a good night's sleep and then head out at dawn to his next destination. The routine had become so familiar that there were times when he even forgot the city in which he was staying.

Since the economy had gone south, Derek had been working at a frantic pace to keep his family's business well in the black. The Perryman was one of thirty-seven luxury hotels the Nolan family owned around the world and it had become his job to make sure they were all operating at peak efficiency. Though he found a lot of satisfaction in doing his job, he'd begun to realize that working sixteen-hour days didn't leave much time for fun.

Just that afternoon, he'd found himself daydreaming through a meeting on the hotel's energy costs, his thoughts wandering to the last time he'd really enjoyed himself. Sure, he'd had vacations and women and distractions over the past eight years, but college had really been the last time he'd felt completely free of responsibility—enough that he was able to relax and just let go.

"Are we stuck?" she asked.

"It should be up and running in a minute," he said, rubbing her back to soothe her nerves. "It probably just needs to reset itself."

"And what if it doesn't? Shouldn't we try to get out while we can?"

She turned, her hip brushing up against his groin, and Derek clenched his jaw. Being near a beautiful woman still caused the same physiological response, the same need to possess. But somewhere along the line, he'd stopped surrendering to his impulses. Sure, he had no trouble finding women to share his bed, but lately, he'd been searching for something more.

Could men and women be friends first and lovers second? Though he'd had a number of long-term relationships, Derek hadn't found that one woman who he felt completely comfortable with.

"We're still not moving," she said, her voice tense and her fingers digging into his arm.

"Don't worry," he said softly.

"You don't think it will…" Her voice faded.

"Plummet to the basement?" Derek asked. "No, I don't think so. There are all kinds of safety features on elevators these days. That only happens in horror movies and bad dreams."

"I have that dream all the time," she said. "And it never ends well."

He reached into his pocket and pulled out his Black-Berry. The screen lit up, providing enough light to see the features of her face. "There should be an alarm button," he said. Derek found the button behind a door on the control panel and pushed it. A buzzer sounded in the shaft above their heads.

Then he dialed the number for the front desk. "Hi, this is Derek Nolan. I'm stuck in the elevator with…" He leaned closer to her. "What's your name?"

"Tess," she said. "Tess Robertson."

"With Tess Robertson. Could you call maintenance and have them get us out?"

"Certainly, Mr. Nolan. Right away. I'm so sorry about this. We've been having a lot of trouble with the elevators lately."

"Just get us out," he said calmly. "And call me at this number if there's any problem." He hung up, then turned the light from the screen toward her. "Is there anyone you'd like to call?"

Tess hesitated for a moment, then shook her head. "No. I'm fine."

But she didn't sound fine. She sounded uneasy. Being in a dark, confined space with a stranger would make anyone nervous. "You don't have to worry," he said. "You're safe with me. In fact, you're better off with me. I'm a pretty important guest here. They'll get us out as quickly as they can."

"I'm really not worried," she said. "I mean, not about

you. But the whole 'plunging to the basement' thing is still an issue."

He chuckled. "Why don't we sit down and make ourselves comfortable." Derek held out his hand and she placed her fingers in his as he helped her settle onto the floor. Derek sat down next to her. Then he set the bottle of scotch between them. "What do you think? Should we open it? It's really good stuff. And it may calm your nerves."

Tess shrugged, crossing her legs in front of her and folding her hands in her lap. She forced a smile. "Why not? Maybe it will soften the fall, too?"

"We're not going to fall," Derek insisted. With a grin, he handed her the BlackBerry. "You hold the light." He peeled the foil from around the cap, then twisted it open. "Unfortunately, I don't have any glasses. Some might consider it a crime to drink twelve-year-old scotch right out of the bottle but desperate times call for desperate measures."

"I don't care what some people say," Tess replied. "I've never really liked arbitrary rules." She raised the bottle to him. "To…to the very strong and capable cable that's holding this elevator up." Like an experienced drinker, she tipped the bottle and took a sip, then coughed. "It's good."

Derek reached over and patted her on the back. "Easy there, you don't want to drink too fast."

With a soft laugh, she handed him back the bottle. "Don't worry. I can handle my liquor."

Derek took a swig of the scotch. "So, Tess Robertson.

Since we're stuck here for a while, tell me about yourself. Are you from Nashville?"

She shook her head, her dark hair falling into her face. "No. I live near Lexington, Kentucky. I manage a horse farm. We breed and raise thoroughbreds. For racing."

"You work with horses?"

Tess nodded. "My dad is a trainer. He put me on a horse when I was three and I haven't been off one since then." She smoothed her hands over her skirt. "Yesterday, I was mucking out stables. Today, I'm sipping expensive scotch in a party dress, waiting for my eminent death." Tess reached for the bottle and took another sip. "What about you?"

"My family owns a chain of hotels."

"Hah!" she said with a laugh. "I bet you're sorry you decided to stay at this one."

"I probably shouldn't admit this, but this hotel is one of ours. The one with the broken elevator."

"You own *this* hotel? Sorry. It's very nice."

"I'm here looking after the family interests. Making sure the staff is doing its job. Tomorrow I head down to Puerto Rico to visit another hotel."

"Your job sounds very glamorous," she said.

"So does your job," he said.

Tess shrugged. "Horses can't bring you room service."

It was an odd statement and caused him to chuckle. Was the scotch beginning to take effect? Or was this just the way she was—honest and plainspoken? "I suppose they can't. But you can't ride a hotel. Or race one."

"Very true," she said.

The light on his phone went out, but they continued to talk in the dark, passing the bottle between them.

"You said you were on your way to a party?"

"The owners of the farm are giving a New Year's Eve party. It's an annual event and I was invited."

"And now, you're stuck here with me," he said in an apologetic tone.

"No, it's fine. I'm really not much of a party girl. I can't remember the last time I wore a dress. And it's one of those high-society deals. Half the time, I don't know what they're talking about and the other half, I don't really care." She paused. "Sorry."

"For what?"

"You're probably one of those high-society types, aren't you."

"No. And you're right to want to stay here," he said in a teasing tone. "I hate socializing with snooty people, too. The atmosphere here is so much nicer. And the conversation more interesting." He picked up his Black-Berry and pulled up a song, the melody barely audible, the light illuminating her profile again. "We even have music."

"Maybe this is exactly what I needed," she said with a sigh.

"Really?"

"I have to take a deep breath. Clear my mind."

"I was just thinking the same thing."

He leaned back against the wall of the elevator and smiled. For the first time in a very long time, he found himself completely relaxed. His brain wasn't spinning with thoughts of business. He took a sip of scotch, then handed her the bottle. "I like this," he murmured.

"Me, too," she said softly.

When their shoulders touched, she didn't pull away and Derek felt the warmth of her body seep into his. He had everything he wanted and needed here in this elevator—a beautiful woman to talk to in the dark, a good bottle of scotch and time to relax.

By anyone's standards, he was successful. He had a job that gave him the opportunity to travel the world on a moment's notice, to stay in luxury surroundings, to work at something he truly enjoyed. And he had a social life that most guys his age would kill for. But he felt old, as if the years spent working were starting to take a toll on him.

Derek knew exactly why he threw himself into his job. It made it easier to forget that he didn't have a life beyond work. And not having a real life just made it easier to work harder. He was caught in a vicious circle and he needed a way out. When he was kid, he'd always considered running away as a viable option. But as an adult his options were—

It was the perfect answer. No explanations necessary, no opportunities to reconsider. Just pick up and leave, deal with the consequences later. "Did you ever feel like taking off?" Derek asked. "Just dropping all of your problems and worries and running in the opposite direction?"

"Never," she said. "I've always stayed and worked them out."

"Me, too. But I'm starting to think that every now and then, it might be nice to just go. Run. And don't look back."

"I was supposed to get engaged tonight. At the party."

The news took him by surprise—first, that she seemed so blasé about their predicament and second, that he felt a sliver of envy for the man who was about to claim her as his own. This was crazy! He'd met her only a few minutes before. Yet he was selfish enough to want her to stay here, with him.

"I guess we'd better get you out of here, then," he said.

"No." Her voice was soft and unsure. "I'd rather stay."

She reached for the bottle at the same time he did and their hands touched. The contact was electric and for a moment, neither of them moved. Derek smoothed his fingers over the back of her wrist, imagining the contours in the dark. "With me or inside this elevator?"

"Both," she said.

"All right, then." He grabbed the bottle and held it up. "Another toast. To a rather unconventional meeting. And to the good fortune that put us in this elevator together."

The lights flickered, then came on. Tess held up her hand to the glare, squinting at the sudden change. Derek cursed beneath his breath. Why the hell did the staff have to be so damn efficient?

A knock sounded and then the doors were slowly forced open. The car was stuck between two floors and the maintenance men were standing on the upper floor. "Sorry about the wait," the hotel manager said, bending down to speak to them. "We're bringing a ladder and we'll have you—"

"Don't bother," Derek said. He stepped over to the doors, setting the scotch down in the corner. "Come on, I'll lift you up." He held out his hand and helped Tess to her feet. Slipping his arms around her waist, he gently lifted her up until the maintenance men grabbed her hands. Then Derek boosted himself up and climbed out into the lobby of the fifth floor.

He dusted his hands off on his pants. "Thank you," he said, nodding to the manager. "And don't worry. I'm not going to mention this to anyone."

"Thank you, Mr. Nolan. I appreciate that."

Tess turned and looked back inside the elevator. "We left the scotch."

"Oh, I can get that for you," the manager volunteered.

"No," Derek said. "There's more where that came from."

They both slowly walked toward the door to the stairwell. When they'd regained a bit of the privacy they'd shared in the elevator, Derek turned to her, still holding on to her hand. "So…"

"So…" she said softly, a winsome smile curling her lips. "It was a pleasure, Mr. Nolan."

"Derek," he murmured.

"Derek. It was nice meeting you."

He knew he had to find some way to keep her with him. But she was late for her engagement party. What could he possibly say to convince her to spend the evening with him? "You don't have to go upstairs. You could stay here with me."

"Right here?" she asked.

"Here. The bar. My suite." He paused. "Or we could always run away."

She drew in a deep breath and to his surprise, he watched her consider his invitation. It was clear from the confusion etching her features that she wasn't thrilled with what awaited her upstairs. "I don't expect anything," he assured. "I just want to get out of here and I'd like you to come along. It'll be an adventure, I promise."

"Why me?" she said.

"I don't know. I like the sound of your voice. It relaxes me. And I don't want to go without you."

"Where will we go?"

"I don't know. We'll figure it out."

She smiled, then nodded. "All right. Yes, I'll go with you."

Derek grinned. "All right." He pushed open the door to the stairwell. "We're going up," he said. "It's going to be a hike." Pointing to her shoes, he shook his head. "And those are going to kill you." He turned his back to her. "Hop on."

"You're going to carry me up the stairs?"

"Yes," Derek said. "You don't think I can do it?"

"I'm perfectly capable of walking." She kicked off her shoes, picked them up and handed them to him. "I bet I can beat you to the top." With a laugh, she started up the stairs. Tess was already on the first landing before he'd even moved.

Derek chuckled to himself. Now, this was going to be fun—a woman as beautiful as Tess challenging him to a race in her party dress and bare feet in a hotel stairwell. Either she'd had too much scotch or she was the most charming creature he'd ever met. He intended to spend the rest of the evening figuring out which it was.

2

WHEN THEY GOT TO THE DOOR of his room, they were both out of breath. Tess leaned back against the wall as he slid the key card through the lock. Suddenly it felt as if the weight of the world had been lifted from her shoulders.

It wasn't really right to run away from her doubts and insecurities—or from Jeffrey—but she was tired of always choosing the safe route. From the time she was seven, she'd had to be the responsible one, always doing her best to choose the right path, make the right decision. For once, she wanted to do something impetuous. She wasn't sure what she'd tell Jeffrey or how he'd feel about being stood up. For one night, she could be wild and spontaneous. Tomorrow she'd start the rest of her life, but tonight she'd be the woman she always wanted to be.

Derek pushed open the door and stepped aside, leaning against the wall and gasping for breath. "Man, you are fast."

"You're not one of those guys that always has to win, are you?" Tess asked. "Because we can go back and do it again, and I can pretend to pull up lame on the last flight of stairs."

He laughed, then swept his arm in front of him. "After you, Secretariat," he said.

"Was that a horse joke?"

"A bad attempt at one."

"Very clever. But Secretariat was a stallion. Genuine Risk was a mare and she won the Derby. And placed at Belmont and Pimlico. My horse, Genny, is named after her."

"You're faster than me. You're prettier than me. And you have your own horse. I think I may have found the perfect woman."

Tess strolled into the suite. It was so easy to relax around Derek. She could be herself, say anything that came into her head, something she'd never been able to do around Jeffrey.

The lights were low and through the wide windows on the opposite wall, she could see the far side of the Cumberland River. She walked over and looked down, watching a barge slowly float south with the current. A moment later, he joined her, bracing his hands on the windowsill next to her.

"It's beautiful," she said.

"I've never really liked this hotel," he said. "But I'm beginning to think I might have been wrong. It is beautiful."

"Do you have a home somewhere, or do you just go from hotel to hotel?" she asked, turning to face him.

"I live out of a suitcase," he said, pointing to the packed garment bag lying on the sofa.

Tess waited for him to continue, but he was suddenly silent. His gaze dropped to her mouth and she felt her heart begin to pound in her chest. Was he thinking of kissing her? She hadn't been kissed by anyone other than Jeffrey for over four years. But she wasn't nervous…just curious.

What would it feel like? Would the thrill racing through her right now increase? The anticipation was so delicious, Tess wanted it to last forever. Anticipation was all she could enjoy, after all. She was supposed to be in love with Jeffrey, committed to him.

He leaned closer and she waited, hoping, knowing that it would probably be more wonderful than she could imagine. But then he drew a deep breath and smiled. "Champagne," he murmured. "I'm going to open a bottle of champagne. Would you like something to eat before we leave? Unfortunately, we don't keep the jet stocked."

Tess swallowed hard. She hated flying. "We're going on a jet?"

"Did you think we'd just set out on foot? Or maybe hop on our bicycles? I have a little more style than that."

"I kind of thought we were metaphorically running away. I assumed we'd stay here. Or maybe go out and get some dinner."

"We could do that," Derek said. "But if we're going to run, I figure we should run as fast and as far as we can."

"Yes," she murmured, so caught up in the fantasy that she could think of only one answer. "Let's go. Right now. Where are we going?"

"I assume you're not carrying a passport, so we'll have to go get that first. You do have a passport, don't you?"

Tess nodded. "I've never used it."

He nodded. "Good. Now, where to go? I really don't want to spend the next ten hours on a plane. How about if we fly to the Caribbean? We can be walking on a beach in three, maybe four hours. Does that sound good?"

The thought of escaping to a warm, sunny beach was almost too good to believe. But this was crazy! Derek Nolan was a complete stranger. "I can't just leave the country. I don't have anything to wear."

"Sure we can. We'll send a messenger to pick up your passport for you and they can meet us at the airport in Lexington. And then we'll be on our way. Is there someone who can get the passport for you at your house?"

Tess nodded. "But what if we can't get a flight? We don't have reservations."

"We're taking my private jet," he said. "And my family owns the island, so there won't be any immigration problems. And where we're going, you won't need anything to wear."

Tess's breath caught in her throat. "What does that

mean? I'm not going to run around naked." Although the prospect seemed intriguing, she thought. Why not just cast aside all her inhibitions and go for it? This was her one chance to live without regret.

Derek laughed, shaking his head. "We have plenty of clothes at the house," he said. "And there's a small resort on the other end of the island that has a number of shops. We can buy you something there if you don't find anything that suits you." He paused. "But if you do decide to run around naked, I'm all right with that, too."

"Good to know," Tess said, giving him wary look.

"Just say the word and I'll call for the plane."

"What's the word?" she asked.

"Yes," he murmured. He smoothed his hands over her bare arms. "We'll have fun, I promise. No expectations, no pressure."

Tess held her breath. This is exactly how she had imagined it, the thrill, the excitement, the undeniable attraction. A handsome man and a tantalizing invitation. "I don't know you," she said.

"I'm a good guy. And we won't be flying alone. I'll introduce you to my pilot and if you don't like him, I'll bring you right back to the hotel. But I think you'd really enjoy spending the night sitting on a sandy beach with your toes in the sand, staring up at the stars."

"All right," she said, throwing caution to the wind. When would she ever have an opportunity like this again? Tonight, she'd live a fantasy with this handsome stranger and tomorrow, she'd make a decision about the rest of her life.

"I'll call my pilot," he said.

Tess nodded. "I'm just going to go freshen up."

"The bathroom is through the bedroom," he said, pulling out his cell phone.

She wandered over to the bedroom door, then looked back at him. For all she knew, he could be a homicidal maniac—a serial killer…with a plane and pilot at his beck and call, and his very own string of hotels with managers and maintenance workers who knew him by name.

Tess stepped inside the luxurious bathroom, then sat down on the edge of the whirlpool tub. She pulled her phone from her clutch purse and quickly dialed Alison's cell phone. When her friend picked up, she turned away from the door and spoke softly. "Hi, it's me."

"Hi," Alison said. "What's going on? Did he propose yet? Are you engaged?"

"I haven't seen Jeffrey. On my way up to the party, I got stuck in the elevator with a gorgeous man. Now I'm in his hotel suite and we're going to get on a plane and fly…somewhere. To the Caribbean." She moaned softly. "Please tell me I'm not crazy."

"Are you kidding me? Of course you're crazy. Get out of there right now."

"But I don't want to leave. I feel like I'm in the middle of some Hollywood movie. He has his own plane. He owns hotels, all over the world. He owns this hotel. And he's so funny and nice and he says he doesn't expect any—"

"That's what they all say," Alison interrupted. "Have you had too much to drink?"

"No," she said. "I want to do this, Ali. I want one night of spontaneity and excitement. One night to be someone I'm not. After that, I can marry Jeffrey. One night is all I need."

"You don't even know this guy," Alison said.

"We're not going to be completely alone. There's the pilot. And he told me he'll be a perfect gentleman."

"What are you going to tell Jeffrey?"

"I'll figure out something," she said. "I just know that I can't bring myself to go to that party. I don't want him to ask me to marry him tonight."

"You are crazy," Alison said.

"I know! Isn't it wonderful? I've never been crazy in my life!" She deserved a fantasy just once, Tess reasoned. She'd spent her entire existence waiting for the next disaster to strike. Now she had a chance to let go of all her worries for one night and to really live. She'd become a practical woman who was about to accept the marriage proposal of a very practical man and together, they'd live a practical life. But not until she had this one night of utter fantasy.

"Let me talk to him," Alison said.

"What?"

"You heard me. I want to talk to this guy. Where are

you? I want to meet him right now. If I say he's all right, then you can go."

"I can't—"

"You will or I'll call security and have them find you."

Tess stood and opened the bathroom door. Derek was waiting in the bedroom, a worried look on his face. "Are you all right? You've been in there an awfully long time."

"Here," she said, holding the phone out to him. "My friend Alison wants to talk to you." Tess felt her cheeks warm. This was definitely not part of the fantasy. She shouldn't need to get permission from anyone to run away with a handsome man.

Derek gave her an odd look, then took the phone. "Hi," he said. For a long time he listened, interjecting a 'yes' every now and then. And finally he gave Alison their room number, said goodbye and handed the phone back to Tess. "She's a little scary. Does she always screen your dates?"

"No. Only those who want to fly me out of the country on a private jet."

He nodded. "Good to have a friend like that. Hey, she can come with us if she wants. You can invite as many people as you like. We can make a party of it."

A knock sounded and Tess followed Derek into the sitting room. Alison was waiting at the door, with a handsome man standing behind her, dressed in faded jeans and a T-shirt. Derek let them both in, introducing himself.

"This is Drew Phillips," Alison said. "Drew, my mentally deranged best friend, Tess Robertson."

Drew sent Tess an apologetic smile. He was almost as handsome as Derek, Tess mused. But not quite.

"It's a pleasure to meet you," Drew said. He turned to Alison. "Why am I here?" he whispered. He turned back to Derek. "Sorry about this. I was just watching the hockey game and she dragged me down here."

"No problem. Hey, would you like to come along with us?" Derek offered. "There's plenty of room in the plane. We're going down to my family's island in the Caribbean. Good food, good weather…good company?"

Alison forced a smile, then grabbed Tess and pulled her into the privacy of the bedroom. When the door was shut behind them, she gave Tess a shrewd look. "Are you drunk?"

"I've had a little scotch," Tess said. "But I'm not drunk. Although I feel…lightheaded. What do you think? Isn't he gorgeous?"

"Yes, he's gorgeous. And he seems like a really nice guy. But you can't be serious about running off with him."

"Why not? He's offering us a free trip to the Caribbean. The last vacation I had was a day at Disneyland when my dad and I were living in California. I was fourteen. If you're worried, come along." Tess sighed. "Haven't you ever done something completely spontaneous?"

"No," Alison said. She shook her head. "All right. Yes. I slept with Drew about twelve hours after I met him. But that was different. I spent the night in his cabin up in the mountains and there was a storm and the road was washed out and…one thing led to another. You're supposed to be getting engaged to Jeffrey."

"And just an hour ago, you were trying to convince me that I needed to find a man who made my heart race," Tess said, grabbing Alison's hand and pressing against her chest. "Feel that? It's racing."

Alison glanced over her shoulder at the closed door. "If you go, then I want some assurance that he'll bring you back in one piece." She opened the door to the bedroom and called Derek inside.

"Give me your wallet," she said.

Derek regarded her suspiciously, but then pulled his wallet out of his jacket pocket and handed it to her. They both watched as Alison rifled through the contents. "You can always see inside a man's soul by going through his wallet." She pulled out a photo of a girl. "Who is this? Your wife?"

"My sister," he said. "Chloe. That's her on her twenty-first birthday."

Alison pulled out a black American Express card. "I suppose you use this to purchase the services of call girls?"

Derek chuckled. "No. I've never been with a call girl. At least, not that I know of."

She held up a condom. "What's this?"

"I think you know what that is," Derek said. "It's always a good idea to be prepared. I'm a guy who believes in being safe."

"Good guy," Drew commented from the door of the bedroom.

Alison gave him a cool look. "All right," she replied. "Well, I think Tess should keep the condom." She closed the wallet and waved it under his nose. "If you do anything to hurt my friend, I will hunt you down and relieve you of the manparts that make that condom necessary. I want her back on Monday morning at the latest."

Tess stepped between them, grabbing Derek's wallet and handing it back to him. "Enough." She drew Alison toward the door. "I'll call you when I get there, I promise. I have my cell phone."

"What are you going to tell Jeffrey?"

"I'll figure that out when he calls," she said. Tess threw her arms around Alison's neck and gave her a hug.

"I still think you're crazy," Alison muttered.

Tess grinned. "I know. But it feels so good."

DEREK GLANCED AT THE SEAT next to him and watched as Tess slept, her head resting on his shoulder. He bent close and drew a deep breath, letting the scent of her perfume tease at his nose.

After jumping through a few hoops, he'd managed to get her on the plane and off the ground. She wasn't keen on flying, worried about the size of the plane and only having one pilot on board. But Derek had assured her that he was a licensed pilot and could land the plane if their pilot dropped dead.

She spent the first half hour on edge, questioning

every sound and bump. Then, after a few glasses of champagne, she'd kicked off her shoes, curled up in one of the large leather seats, and dozed off. He smiled to himself, reluctant to wake her. Derek relished the chance to look at her freely.

He hadn't noticed before, but she had the most perfect mouth, in the shape of a Cupid's bow. How would it feel to kiss that mouth, he wondered. Though he'd assured her he had no expectations, that didn't stop him from thinking about seducing her. After all, he did find her incredibly attractive. And the more he got to know her, the more interested he became.

What kind of woman would walk away from her engagement party and get on a plane with a complete stranger? Except for her habit of saying whatever popped into her mind, she didn't seem like the impulsive sort. Yet, here she was, running away to paradise with him. She hadn't revealed much about herself, beyond the fact that she managed a horse farm, that she'd moved around a lot as a kid and that she was about to marry the boss's son.

But he saw something in her eyes, in the way her brow furrowed while she was making the decision to escape. It was as if his offer had lifted the weight of the world from her shoulders. It wasn't just a marriage proposal she was trying avoid. That could have been settled with a simple "no." Derek suspected there was something else, something much deeper that was pulling her down.

Everyone had at least a few secrets, he mused. His

love life hadn't been a bed of roses. Five years ago, he'd been ready to consider marriage. But after a prolonged engagement, his fiancée, an interior designer working out of their corporate offices, dumped him—for his older brother, Sam. Since then, every family gathering was an exercise in awkwardness for Derek.

He turned to stare out the window of the Lear jet, searching for the lights of the landing strip at Angel Cay. His family had owned the island in the Caribbean since his grandfather had bought it forty years ago. At the time, his board of directors had fought the purchase. Back then, it had been little more than a small patch of sand and scrub northwest of Abaco. But over the years, the island had become a pet project of his grandfather's and he'd turned it into a lush, tropical paradise with palm trees and gardens and white clapboard buildings.

He'd designed a beautiful plantation house, built to weather the hurricanes. The airstrip had been lengthened to accommodate small jets ten years ago and private cottages had been added on the north end of the island, creating an exclusive resort popular with the Hollywood crowd.

Though the cottages were probably booked, Derek knew the main house was empty. His family was spending the holidays at their newest hotel in Bermuda, Sam and Alicia included. Derek had left them there the day after Christmas, making his excuses that he was needed for a week of meetings at some of the U.S. properties.

Though he'd been prepared to greet the New Year alone, in a comfortable suite somewhere, Derek was glad he'd chosen to enter a balky elevator. He wasn't quite sure what he was doing with Tess or where their time together would lead, but from the moment he'd set eyes on her, he'd decided not to waste too much time thinking about it.

Derek reached out and touched her knee. "Hey," he whispered. "Tess. Wake up."

She opened her eyes, then frowned, taking in her surroundings. At first, it seemed as if she didn't know where she was, but then she stared straight at him. "Is there something wrong with the plane?"

"No. But we're going to be landing soon."

"Too much champagne," she murmured, stretching her arms over her head. "And no sleep last night."

His eyes took in the smooth expanse of her shoulders and the soft flesh of her breasts above the deeply cut neckline. Drawing a ragged breath, he ignored the desire racing through him. He'd made a promise to her and he intended to keep it—no matter how difficult it was. "You need to put on your seat belt."

She straightened and searched for the ends of the belt, but fumbled with fastening it. Derek slid out of his seat and knelt down in front of her to help. As she leaned forward, they bumped heads. He glanced up to find her lush lips just inches from his and the impulse to kiss her was impossible to deny.

He brushed his lips against hers and her breath seemed to catch in her throat. Time seemed to stand still, the soft roar of the engines lulling them both into a quiet contemplation of what had just happened.

Derek had never put a whole lot of thought into kissing a woman. It normally just happened in the course of events. But with Tess, there was much more at stake. One kiss could be the end of their time together. One kiss and she might demand that he turn the plane around and take her home.

But like a tantalizing flavor he couldn't resist, Derek took another taste, this time tracing the crease of her mouth with his tongue. A tiny sigh slipped from her throat as her lips parted and he took the reaction as an invitation and deepened the kiss.

Bracing his hands on either side of her body, he pressed her back into the soft leather seat. There was nothing in her response that told him to stop. If anything, she seemed curious to explore further. Her hand rested on his chest and he knew she could feel his heart pounding through the fabric of his shirt.

Derek smoothed his hand along the length of her leg, her skin like silk beneath his fingers. The fabric of her skirt rustled as he slid beneath it. He didn't know her, yet the attraction to her was so intense, he could barely control himself.

Though he tried to tell himself that kissing her was enough, the process of slowly seducing her was what intrigued him the most. Each word between them, each glance, each touch took them further down that road. They'd started at square one in the elevator, two complete strangers sharing a drink in the dark. And now a few hours later, they were moving closer and closer to surrender.

When he finally drew back and looked down at her, her face was flushed and her lips damp. He held his breath, waiting for her protest, but it never came. "I have to go up to the cockpit," he murmured. He fastened her seat belt, then stood up in front of her, taking a deep breath and willing his heartbeat to slow down.

"Is there something wrong with the pilot?" she asked.

"He hasn't done a night landing on Angel Cay before and I have. It can be tricky. I'll be back in a few minutes."

Derek made his way to the cockpit and slipped into the copilot's seat. Jeremy Nichols, one of the corporation's best pilots, was behind the controls for this flight. He'd been more than happy to leave Nashville early, especially for a two-day layover in the Caribbean.

"You'll want to circle around and come in from the west. There's usually a pretty stiff breeze from the east. The runway is 5500 feet. Touch down between the blue lights and you'll have plenty of room."

"Got it," Jeremy said. He glanced over at Derek. "So, who is the girl? I thought you were planning on spending New Year's weekend hard at work."

Derek chuckled. "Do you blame me for changing my mind?"

"She's pretty. Where did you find her?"

"In an elevator." He grinned, his gaze scanning the instruments. "I don't know. There's something about her. We were sitting in the dark and her voice just drew me in. It's like I know this girl, but we're complete strangers."

"Well, I'm happy you met her. I won't mind spending the next few days lying on a beach and working on my tan."

"I thought I'd send you back to San Diego," Derek teased.

"No!" Jeremy said.

"Kidding. The pool house will be empty. You can sleep there."

"And where is the girl going to sleep?"

"Wherever she wants," Derek said. "We have plenty of bedrooms, although I wouldn't be adverse to have her share mine. Now, can we stop talking and land this plane?"

"You got it, boss."

They went through the landing checklist with quiet efficiency and though Jeremy was focused on the job at hand, Derek couldn't keep his thoughts off Jeremy's question. Where would she sleep? Did she think he'd expect her to share his bed? Though he'd made it clear that he'd be a gentleman, there was no denying the attraction between them.

With other women, he'd always been certain of the outcome of an evening. But for once, it felt good not to know. Whatever transpired between the two of them would be a surprise. That would be his New Year's resolution, Derek thought to himself. "Add more spontaneity to my life," he murmured.

"What?" Jeremy said, reaching for the switch that lowered the landing gear.

"Nothing," Derek said. Hell, he'd brought her to one of the most romantic spots in the world. He couldn't help it if the atmosphere had a seductive effect on her.

THEY RODE from the airstrip in a Range Rover, the windows open to the warm night air. Tess sat in back with Derek, feeling a bit uneasy in the company of Jeremy and the driver. What did the two other men think of her? Was she just another in a long line of women that Derek Nolan had brought to this island to seduce? Or were they aware that she and Derek were not romantically involved?

Tess groaned inwardly, her thoughts wandering back to the kiss they'd shared on the plane. She ought to have felt remorseful, yet Tess couldn't muster even the smallest sliver of guilt for what she'd done.

In all the time she'd been with Jeffrey, he'd never once elicited the kind of reaction from her that Derek had managed. She shivered, the memory causing a physical response. It was a delicious kiss and something she'd probably have to explain to Jeffrey—someday.

Though the notion of flying off with a handsome stranger was the stuff of fantasies, she still had to rationalize her decision. Maybe this was the female equivalent of a bachelor party, that one last chance to sow her wild oats, before committing herself to Jeffrey. Besides, though the kiss was wonderful and she'd been a willing participant, Tess hadn't initiated it.

It wasn't the best rationalization, but she had time to work on something better. From now on, she was going to hold Derek to his promise—no expectations. And no more kisses.

The facade of the stucco plantation house was lit up in the dark and she could see it from the long winding driveway. As they approached, Tess realized that it wasn't just a house, but an estate. The main house at Beresford Farms was nice, but this house was truly impressive.

"Wow," she murmured.

"I know," Derek said. "My grandfather started building and he couldn't seem to stop. It's big, but comfortable. You can have a room in the main house or you can have one of the cottages."

"I'm afraid the cottages are all rented, Mr. Nolan," the driver said.

"Then it's the house," Derek replied.

When the Range Rover pulled to a stop, he hopped out and helped her from the car, resting his arm on the small of her back as they approached the wide verandah that circled the building.

The front door burst open and a young woman came running out. She threw herself into Derek's arms. "Oh, you're here! God, I thought I'd have to spend New Year's Eve all alone. Chris couldn't fly in with me and Daddy said I couldn't send one of our pretty little jets to pick him up, so now he's stuck in New York and I'm stuck here. But now I have a jet." She glanced over at Jeremy. "And a pilot, I see." She looked at Tess. Pulling away from Derek, she held out her hand. "I'm Chloe. Derek's sister."

"Chloe, this is Tess. Tess Roberts."

"Robertson," Tess said.

"Right. Robertson. Tess."

"Are you Jeremy's girlfriend?" she asked, looking over at the pilot.

"She's here with me," Derek said.

"Really? Derek never brings company to the island. You must be pretty special." With that, she turned and walked back inside the house. "Come on, Jeremy, I'll feed you and then we're going to get my boyfriend in New York."

"I bet she's a handful," Jeremy muttered, climbing the front steps. When he reached the top, he turned. "Good night. It was a pleasure flying you both." He disappeared through the open front door, leaving Tess and Derek alone.

"Sorry about this," Derek said. "I didn't know she'd be here. I thought we'd have the place to ourselves. But she'll be gone soon enough."

In truth, Tess was glad for the company. Having a chaperone around would keep her from tossing all caution to the wind and behaving badly. "She's your sister," Tess said. "And I don't mind."

He reached out and ran his hands up and down her arms, causing a tremor to race through her. They'd known each other for only four hours, yet she'd already begun to crave his touch. His hands were strong, his caress sure, as if he was used to taking what he wanted when he wanted it.

Tess swayed a bit, her knees slowly turning to jelly. As if sensing her thoughts, he pulled her into his arms, letting her body mold to his. Derek's mouth came down on hers in a long, delicious kiss.

No, this wasn't supposed to happen again, she thought to herself as she frantically tried to find a way to stop him. But as the kiss grew more intense, Tess knew that denying their attraction was an exercise in futility. How could she ever have been satisfied with Jeffrey, she wondered. This was real passion.

When he finally drew back, she looked up at him. "We shouldn't do that," Tess murmured.

He blinked as if surprised by her statement. "But I thought you enjoyed—"

"That's not the point," Tess explained. "I'm…engaged. Or almost engaged."

"But you did enjoy it," he said, leaning close to whisper the words into her ear.

"Yes," she replied in a strangled voice. "But I don't want you to think that there will be more." Oh, who was she kidding? She couldn't deny the desire that welled up inside of her every time their mouths met. Alison was right. She'd been crazy to accept his invitation. Every minute she spent in Derek Nolan's arms just made it more impossible for her to consider marriage to Jeffrey.

"All right," he said, smoothing his hand along her hip. "No more kissing."

"No more touching," Tess said.

He pulled his hand away. "All right. But if you kiss me, I can't be held responsible for enjoying it." He grabbed her hand and pulled her along into the house, already ignoring her request. "I promised you sand between your toes. Come on. I'll show you your room and then we'll go down to the beach."

As they hurried through the house, Tess took in the luxurious surroundings. This evening was becoming more and more surreal. She was just an ordinary girl, used to spending her nights with her nose buried in paperwork and her days with her feet buried in straw. She knew people lived like this and had even witnessed it from the sidelines, but she'd never realized how alluring it all was.

The house was like something out of a travel magazine. It was built in a French plantation style, a U-shaped structure with a courtyard garden in the middle, complete with fountain. All of the rooms opened onto the courtyard with tall French doors replacing windows, which were thrown open to catch the ocean breeze. Tess could smell the sea in the air and hear the distant waves.

They walked along a wide verandah, chairs and tables scattered between huge potted palms. She passed a hanging basket, draped with some type of exotic flower and the scent was like perfume. Tess drew another deep breath, trying to memorize every aspect of this night. She half expected to open her eyes and find out she was dreaming.

When they reached the end of the verandah, they climbed the stairs to the second story and Derek led her through a set of French doors into a dimly lit room. It was dominated by a huge four-poster bed, which had been draped in mosquito netting and covered in expensive bed linens.

"I hope this is all right," he said, shrugging out of his jacket and tossing it over the arm of an overstuffed chair. He pulled his loosened tie over his head and yanked his shirttails out of his pants. "The bathroom is over there. If you need anything, you can dial 'seven' and the concierge at the resort will take care of you. I'll make sure that Chloe finds you something to wear before she leaves."

Tess watched him as he unbuttoned the front of his shirt, revealing deeply tanned and muscular chest. This was going to be so much more difficult than she ever expected. Her fingers twitched and she imagined the feel of his skin beneath her fingers. What she was contemplating could be considered infidelity. Could? It *was* infidelity!

He frowned. "What?"

"You're getting undressed," she said.

Derek stopped, then chuckled softly. "I'm just getting comfortable before we walk down to the beach," he said. "Sorry. This place brings out the bohemian in me."

Tess felt her cheeks warm in embarrassment. "No, that's fine. I thought that…well, never mind."

"I'll say it again," he murmured as he crossed the room. "Nothing will happen unless you want it to."

"Why did you bring me here?" Tess asked, her curiosity getting the better of her. If it wasn't for sex, then what was it?

He thought about her question for a long moment, then shrugged. "I'm not sure. I just didn't want to let you go. I find you…intriguing."

This brought a laugh from Tess. His confession was ridiculous. Intriguing was the last word she'd use to describe herself. Maybe she had finally managed to acquire an air of mystery. Or maybe she was just weird enough to pique his curiosity.

"It's not that complicated." Derek gave her arm a squeeze. "Why don't you settle in and I'll go down to the kitchen and grab us something to drink. Then we'll go out to the beach. I'll order dinner, too."

He walked out the door, leaving Tess to her thoughts. She sat down on the end of the bed and shook her head. Nothing would happen unless she wanted it to. In truth, had Derek continued to undress, she would have been sorely tempted to tear off her own clothes the moment he was naked.

They both could sense the desire between them and they both knew exactly where it could lead. But there was a line she couldn't cross, a point of no return. If she expected to return home and marry Jeffrey, then she'd have to behave herself and put those feelings aside. A few careless kisses were easy to forgive. But a full-on completely naked sexual encounter wasn't. Derek had promised her a tropical vacation and that's exactly what she needed before moving on with her life.

"Just enjoy it while it lasts," she said softly. All of it. For it was a rare occasion when a fantasy actually became reality.

3

"YOU'RE JUST FULL of surprises. Have you ever brought a girlfriend here?" his sister asked.

Derek glanced over his shoulder from his spot in front of the kitchen wine cooler, then grabbed a bottle of champagne. "She's not my girlfriend. She's just a friend. More of an acquaintance, actually." he said.

"Yeah, that little mix-up with the name was embarrassing, wasn't it?" Chloe said. "I always thought you were Mr. Smooth with the ladies."

"Is there a reason you've decided to bust my balls or do you just have nothing else to do?"

Chloe boosted herself up on the edge of the granite countertop. "How long are you staying?"

"I don't know. The night. Maybe the entire weekend. But I want you out of here tonight. Jeremy will fly you and that boyfriend of yours wherever you want. Just don't come back here."

"If she's just a friend, why the need to be completely alone?" Chloe asked.

He turned and sent her an impatient glare. "I don't have to explain myself to you."

Chloe held her hands up in mock surrender. "Hey, I'm just saying this is a good thing. Maybe it's time you forgot what happened with Alicia and move on with your life." His sister jumped off the counter. "She seems like a nice person. Although not really your type."

"What is my type?" he asked.

"I don't know. Kind of plastic. You know, so beautiful it makes your teeth hurt. And makes your little sister feel like an ugly duckling."

"Tess is beautiful," Derek said.

"She is. But she's also real. I think that's actually her natural hair color. And I'm pretty sure nothing else on her is fake."

"She is real," Derek murmured. "I like that about her."

"Then don't do anything to screw it up." Chloe stood next to him and placed a quick kiss on his cheek. She strolled over to the stairs. "I'm going to pack and then I'll be gone. Who knows what might happen when you two are alone?"

Derek smiled to himself as he watched her leave. Twenty-three-year-old Chloe was the youngest of the four Nolan siblings and by far the most trouble. Almost seven years younger than Derek, she'd been the baby of the family—a spoiled rotten baby. But she'd been the only one who'd taken his side in the whole Alicia affair.

His parents had urged him to accept Alicia's duplicity

as the course of true love and be happy for his older brother. His older sister, Kara, never one to rock the boat, had sided with their parents. But Chloe had never really trusted Alicia and her instincts had been spot on.

Derek grabbed a pair of champagne flutes from the cabinet, then headed outside. He'd ordered a light dinner from the resort kitchen to be delivered to his favorite spot on the beach. The small resort, situated on the opposite end of the island operated independently of the main house, with its own reception area, kitchen and small restaurant to serve the ten bungalows. The shared staff was employed to cater to the guests' every whim and they did their work quietly and efficiently.

He found Tess sitting on the edge of her bed, her hands folded in her lap. Leaning against the doorjamb, he held up the champagne, then showed her the glasses he'd brought. "No more drinking out of the bottle," he murmured.

She shrugged. "I don't mind. I'm not the fancy type."

"I like that about you," he said. "You don't pretend to be something you're not. Come on, let's walk down to the beach and get your toes wet." He handed her the bottle and glasses, then bent down and slipped her shoes off her feet. Then he kicked off his own, pulled off his socks and rolled his pants. "There. We're officially on vacation." Derek pointed to the French doors that lined the outside wall of her room. "Through there," he said.

The beach was about one hundred yards beyond the

back of the house. A lighted path wound through the sea grass and they followed it down a small hill and out onto a wide swath of sand. Tess stopped and turned back to Derek. "It's lovely." She tipped her face up to the moon and drew a deep breath.

"Yeah, it's not bad," he agreed. "Running away from life is a lot easier when you have a place like this to go to."

They strolled near the water's edge in comfortable silence. Derek didn't feel the need to make idle conversation with her. The typical flirtatious games hadn't been a part of their meeting and now, it didn't seem like they were necessary. "I've only seen the ocean…three times," she said.

"This isn't technically an ocean," he said. "It's a sea."

"It's the same water as the ocean, right?"

"Yeah, it all runs together." He glanced over at her. "What oceans did you see?"

"The Pacific twice. We lived in California for a while and my dad took me. We had to take three different buses because we'd sold our truck to pay for groceries. And it was raining. But we had fun."

"What about your mom?"

"She left when I was young. She just couldn't stand the lifestyle, moving from place to place. She just…ran away one day and didn't come back. She tried to contact me a few years ago, but I didn't want to see her."

"I'm sorry," he murmured. He hadn't meant to bring up bad memories. And his first instinct was to yank her into his arms and kiss away his mistake. He stepped closer, hoping that she'd feel the need for physical contact. But she just smiled and shook her head.

"There's nothing to be sorry about. It just wasn't for her. And I had an interesting life with my dad. I learned everything about horse breeding and training from him and now I run the farm. I'm one of the youngest managers around."

"This is it," Derek said.

A large chaise sat in the sand with lanterns dangling from poles behind it, their flames flickering in the breeze. A wicker picnic hamper waited on a nearby table along with a pitcher of rum drinks that the chef had provided for a beverage. "You did all this?" she asked, picking up a rum punch, decorated with fresh fruit.

"No," Derek said. "I had them send it over from the resort. But it was my idea. Does that count?"

She walked over to the chaise and plopped down, tossing her purse into the sand. Stretching her arm over her head, Tess sighed. "No wonder rich people work so hard to keep their money. It buys you comforts like this," she said before taking a long sip of her punch.

Derek slid onto the other side of the chaise and set the champagne in the sand. "You like it?"

"What's not to like?" Tess said. "Although I feel like I should have someone here to feed me grapes and massage my feet."

"That can be arranged," he said.

"You have foot massagers on staff?"

"I think I could handle that on my own. May I?"

She nodded and Derek grabbed her bare foot and began to rub it gently. She wriggled down into the cushions, her gaze fixed on his hands. He was good at reading signals and his touch was definitely having an effect on her.

"Those shoes were like instruments of torture," she murmured. "I usually spend my day in worn-out riding boots." He moved his thumbs to the arch of her foot. "Oh, that feels good," she said, closing her eyes. "No one has ever massaged my feet before."

"I'm glad I could be your first," Derek said. He drew her foot up and pressed a kiss on the inside of her ankle. "That doesn't count, by the way. It's part of the massage."

She playfully pulled her foot away from his grasp. "I'm not sure you can be trusted."

Derek captured her foot again and resumed his task. "I can always be trusted." He smoothed his hands along her calf and then back down to her foot again. "So, since this guy is the one standing between me and your lips, maybe you should tell me about him."

She shook her head. "I don't want to talk about him," Tess replied.

"If that elevator had worked properly, you'd be at the party now." His fingers continued to knead at the tension in her foot and she moaned softly. "Wouldn't you?"

"I don't know. He really didn't have anything to do with my decision to run away. That was all me." She raised her other foot, wiggling her toes beneath his chin. "Now this one."

Derek grabbed her foot and pressed the arch to his mouth. "You're very demanding." His lips moved higher, to her ankle. "There will have to be some reciprocation here."

"What does that mean?"

"I rub your feet, you rub mine?" He moved higher still, bracing his arms on either side of her body and looking directly into her eyes. He leaned in, but stopped when his lips were nearly touching hers. "If you really loved the guy, you wouldn't be here with me," he whispered.

His observation brought a quiet shift in her mood and she grew pensive. "I know."

Derek didn't move, afraid that he'd made a huge mistake. And then she wriggled out from beneath him and he knew he had.

"Maybe I shouldn't be here," she murmured, standing beside the chaise. "You brought up a very important question. What am I doing here? I'm putting everything I've worked for at risk." She spun on her heel and strode toward the water, then suddenly turned back, her drink sloshing out of her glass. "When he finds out about this, he's going to be furious. I mean, right now he probably just thinks I'm caught in traffic. Or maybe he's calling the hospitals, wondering if I've been in some kind of accident." She hurried back to Derek and grabbed her purse. "I'll call him. I'll make up some story. And then you have to take me back."

"Tess, wait." Derek cursed beneath his breath. He should have known this would happen. He'd pushed her a little too far a little too fast. "Come on, Tess, let's just back up here." The first interesting woman he'd met in months and she got an attack of the guilts.

"Back up? How is that possible? God, how could I have been so stupid?"

She shoved the rum punch at him and he grabbed it, biting back another curse. "All right. Whatever you want," Derek said softly. "I'll take you back."

"Right," she said, staring at the screen of her cell phone. "Whatever I want." She walked away again, obviously needing privacy in order to make her excuses. Derek watched her in the moonlight, the ocean breeze whipping at her hair and her dress.

He wanted to grab her phone and throw it into the ocean. He wanted to pull her into his arms and kiss her again, erasing any fears or doubts she had, obliterating the image of that guy from her mind. But he'd made a promise and though every instinct told him to break it, he liked Tess a little too much to deliberately defy her.

A low roar sounded in the distance and a few seconds later, he saw the lights from the Lear jet rising in the eastern sky. Chloe was on her way back to the States. And now he and Tess were without transportation off the island. They were stuck here, at least for the night.

All in all, the trip was worth the trouble, Derek rationalized. He'd discovered one important thing. There were still women in the world who had the capacity to intrigue him. And yet he wondered if he'd ever meet a woman quite like Tess again.

TESS STARED DOWN at the text message that had been waiting for her when she turned on the phone. She shook her head, then reread it, certain she'd misunderstood.

Jeffrey Beale announced his engagement to Denise Simpson-Graves at the party tonight. Call me ASAP.

The text was from Alison and had been posted more than an hour ago. Jeffrey was engaged? To a woman she'd never heard of? How could that be? She gave the phone a shake, certain that the message had gotten jumbled by the distance. But there it was, in black and white. Jeffrey had announced his engagement to another woman.

Tess felt emotion surge up inside her, a bitter mix of shock and anger. Was this the announcement he'd told her about? How could she have been so blind? How could she have thought *she* was supposed to be the woman on the receiving end of that engagement ring?

Sure, her relationship with Jeffrey hadn't been public, but she'd never even suspected his reasons for keeping it secret had to do with another woman. Suddenly little clues began to fall into place. Maybe he hadn't even known she'd been invited to the party. Maybe the invitation had come from his parents. Jeffrey hadn't invited his future fiancée, his parents had invited their farm manager. She'd just assumed

Drawing a deep breath, Tess texted back a single word. Thanks. She waiting, staring at the screen, hoping that Alison was there at the other end. And then the phone vibrated softly, alerting her to an incoming text. You okay?

Just fine, Tess texted back, adding a smiley face to the end of the sentence. "Just fine," she repeated to herself. After all, wasn't this what she wanted? She'd been ready to run back home just a few minutes ago. And now, lying, cheating Jeffrey Beale had saved her the trouble. Thank God he had, Tess mused. Imagine the embarrassment, no, the humiliation, had she been there at the party when he'd made his announcement.

How could she have been so blind? So stupid? A sudden realization struck her. Oh, God, maybe there never had been a real romance. Maybe Tess had always just been his "girl on the side." Or maybe he had planned this all. And by inviting her to the party, he'd been signaling an end to their relationship and issuing a warning at the same time—if she wanted to keep her job, she'd keep her mouth shut.

"Is everything all right?"

Tess snapped around at the sound of Derek's voice. "Yes," she said, her voice wavering. "Everything is great. I could use another rum punch though. Or six or seven."

"I thought you wanted me to take you home."

She stepped up to him, her gaze fixed on his. Then she wrapped her arms around his neck and kissed him, long and deep, hoping that she might erase the memory of her one-minute meltdown. There was no reason now not to discard the last of her inhibitions and enjoy her vacation.

Now she knew why she'd left that elevator with Derek instead of going upstairs to Jeffrey. Somewhere, deep inside her heart, she'd harbored doubts about Jeffrey Beale and his motives. And though she hadn't been conscious of this, some primal instinct to protect herself had kicked in.

"We just got here," she said. "Why would I want to leave now?"

Tess returned to the chaise and tossed her phone onto the cushion, then accepted the glass from Derek. "I'm in the mood to celebrate."

"Don't drink that too fast—it will go to your head," Derek warned.

Tess closed her eyes and tipped her face up to the sky. "Oh, I hope so," she said with a sigh. For a long moment she studied him. "You really are beautiful," she murmured, her eyes drifting to his sculpted lips.

"Thank you," he said with a soft chuckle. "So are you."

Tess tipped her head to the side, then felt a bit dizzy and reached for his shoulder. "Do you think I'm more beautiful than Denise Simpson-Graves?"

"I don't know Denise Simpson-Graves," he said.

She pasted a bright smile on her face. "Neither do I."

"But my answer is still yes."

Tess reached out and touched her fingertips to his lower lip. "Maybe you should kiss me again." She'd never been bold with men, especially when it came to her own needs. But here, away from the real world, she could forget the ordinary girl she'd become and focus on the woman who had the capacity to seduce a man like Derek.

Maybe it was the warm ocean breeze. Maybe it was the moonlight gleaming off the water. Or maybe it was the adrenaline pumping through her after her recent humiliation. But in this fantasy, she wasn't afraid to act on her impulses and take exactly what she wanted from him.

Derek toyed with a strand of her hair as his gaze slowly drifted along the length of her body. "So we're rid of the rules now?"

"No rules," she murmured, shaking her head.

"Then tell me exactly what you want and I'll give it to you." He leaned over and pressed his lips to her shoulder. "There's this."

"That will do," she said.

He moved up to gently nibble at her neck. "And this."

"That's even better."

When he finally reached her mouth, Tess's heart was pounding so hard she could barely hear him speak. "And this." He slipped his arm around her waist and pulled her beneath him, his lips coming down on hers in a kiss that was both gentle and demanding.

Tess felt as if her body was melting into his, the heat from his bare chest seeping through her dress and into her skin. Suddenly, she wanted to rid herself of all her clothes. She wanted to feel what it would be like between them once they'd gone past the point of no return.

His lips drifted downward again, to her neck and then lower, to the spot of cleavage between her breasts. She arched against him, inviting him to go further, to brush aside the strap to her gown and expose another few inches of skin. But Derek seemed determined to take his time, returning to her mouth again for another kiss.

As she lost herself in the taste of his lips, Tess closed her eyes. But the effects of the rum punch were sinking in and her head spun. Then, the entire chaise seemed to start spinning. Tess threw out her arms, trying to regain her equilibrium.

"Wait," she said.

Derek pushed up, staring at her in confusion. "Wait as in stop? Or slow down?"

"Wait until the chaise stops spinning," Tess said.

He shook his head, then stood. "Why don't we walk it off? You drank that punch a little fast."

He reached out, pulling her to her feet. Lacing his fingers through hers, he drew her to the water's edge.

As Tess stared out at the sea, she felt an undeniable urge to wash away every memory of Jeffrey. It would be like a baptism, a rebirth. From this moment on, she'd begin a new life, one full of a passion and spontaneity and fun. She wouldn't think things over carefully before acting, she'd just trust her instincts. Pulling Derek along with her, she waded in up to her knees.

"It's so warm," she said.

"Not that warm," he said, staying in ankle-deep water.

"If you don't want to get your pants wet, take them off." Tess laughed, then spun around in the shallows, dipping her hands in as she turned. "Don't you feel like tearing your clothes off and taking a swim?" In truth, that was exactly how she felt. She wanted to enjoy the sensation of the warm water enveloping her body. She walked a little farther out, her skirt billowing out around her, her gaze fixed on the horizon as the moon dipped a bit lower.

Suddenly, he was behind her, his hand gripping her waist. "Be careful," he murmured. "The surf can sweep you off your feet."

She turned around, wrapped her arms around his neck and kissed him, her mouth lingering, her tongue teasing. "Did anyone ever tell you that you're a really nice guy?"

"If you knew what was running through my head right now, you wouldn't say that."

"Bad thoughts?" Tess asked.

"Not bad. Naughty. Very, very naughty."

She leaned into him. "Tell me. I want to know."

"I'm thinking about the sound the zipper on the back of your dress will make as I pull it down. I'm thinking about the underwear you're wearing—or maybe not wearing—beneath that dress. I'm wondering what it would feel like to touch you…everywhere. Anywhere."

"You'll have to catch me first!" Tess turned and

started for the shore. But the surf knocked her off balance and in the blink of an eye, she'd fallen, sinking beneath the surface. Her skirt tangled around her thighs and she struggled to right herself. Then she felt his hand on her arm as Derek pulled her to her feet.

Coughing and sputtering, she held on to him until he lost his balance and they both tumbled back into the water. By they time they both managed to struggle to the shore, Tess was coughing up salt water and Derek was patting her on the back.

"I warned you," he said.

The salt water in her nose caused her to sneeze, once and then again. Flopping back into the sand, she took a deep breath and then began to laugh, her predicament suddenly more ridiculous than embarrassing. "My head is suddenly very clear."

Derek stretched out beside her, his head braced on his hand. "You've had a busy night."

He looked so handsome with his hair slicked back and droplets of water clinging to his lashes. Tess reached up and smoothed her fingers along his temple. How was it that she felt closer to this stranger than she had to the man she thought she'd eventually marry? "Maybe we should get out of these wet clothes," she whispered.

It was clear by the expression on his face that he knew what she wanted. And when he stood and helped her to her feet, she also knew that what was about to happen would wipe the last memories of Jeffrey Beale from her mind. The real fantasy was about to begin.

"I think that's a very good idea," Derek said.

DEREK LINGERED over her mouth, his tongue softly probing, meeting hers in a delicious dance. He wove his fingers through her tangled hair, breathing softly against her lips.

They stood on the verandah outside her room, light spilling out of the open French doors into the darkness. Neither one of them was ready to venture inside just yet. Their clothes were wet and sand clung to every bit of exposed skin and damp fabric.

Her dizziness had passed and Tess was relaxed and happy and pliant in his arms. Derek wrapped his arm around her waist and drew her into a slow dance, humming a soft tune as he did. He nuzzled her neck. "So, if there are no rules, which one should we break first?"

"There are so many to choose from," Tess teased. "Let me think. We could get some scissors and run around with them in our hands?"

"I didn't know you were such a danger junkie," Derek said. "You like to live on the edge."

"I do," Tess said. "I ran away with you, didn't I?"

"Do you think I'm dangerous?" he asked.

Tess nodded. "A little. Or maybe I'm just dangerous when I'm with you."

"Tell me what you really want to do," Derek insisted.

"I really want to take off my clothes," she said. "The sand is starting to itch and I just want to be dry and warm."

"I can help you with that," he said.

She chuckled softly. "Yes, I imagine you could." Tess

turned away from him and leaned against the railing, spreading her arms wide. "Go ahead. Get me out of these clothes."

Derek smoothed his hands over her shoulders and down her arms. He'd been thinking about this all night long and now, she'd offered him exactly what he wanted. Reaching out, he grabbed the zipper and slowly drew it down, revealing bare skin.

He slipped his hands beneath the fabric and she held on to the front of the bodice as he circled her waist. Her skin was cool and her body soft. A flood of desire rushed through him and as he bent close and kissed her shoulder, he felt himself growing hard.

His first impulse was to pick her up and carry her into her bedroom. They could be completely naked in a matter of seconds, but after that, they'd have to stop. He hadn't brought any protection and the condom her friend Alison had confiscated was still in Tess's purse down on the beach. It would probably be better to hit the "pause" button sooner rather than later. He gently turned her to face him.

"Are we going to do this?" she asked.

"Do you want to?"

Tess nodded, her eyes wide, her lips parted. Derek could see that she was nervous and he wanted to give her time to change her mind. But when she reached up and ran her fingers over his chest, he knew that there was no reason to wait.

He groaned softly as he wrapped his arms around her waist and pulled her body against his, his mouth coming down on hers. He'd been waiting for this all night—in truth, from the moment she'd stepped into the elevator. But Derek knew once they began, they wouldn't be able to stop. And he wasn't quite prepared for what was going to happen.

"I have to go back to my room," he murmured. "Why don't you jump in the shower and rinse off all that sand. I'll join you when I get back."

"I'll be here," Tess said.

"I'll be back."

By the time he got downstairs and crossed the courtyard, he could see her moving around her room. He stood in the darkness, the night breeze cool against his skin, and watched her. She had discarded her dress and underwear and her naked body was outlined by the soft light from the lamps in her room, the details obscured by distance.

Derek sucked in a sharp breath, need pulsing through his body. What stroke of fate had made him hold that elevator for her? Just a few seconds later and they would have passed each other by, never knowing the other existed. But now here they were, together, and the possibilities for the night were still spinning out in front of him.

When he got to his room, he stripped out of his damp trousers, ran a towel over his sandy skin, then pulled on a pair of board shorts. He found a box of condoms in his shaving kit and shoved them in his pocket, then jogged back out to the verandah and down the stairs.

As he walked back to her room, an image of her swam

in his head. She was naked, standing in the shower, the water running over her body. Derek could almost feel her flesh beneath his touch, could taste her mouth and hear her soft sighs.

When he walked through the open doors of her room, the light was off. He tripped over her damp dress, left in heap on the floor. Behind the mosquito net draped over her bed, he saw a silhouette of a figure. He crossed the room and pulled back the netting.

Tess was curled up beneath the sheet, her damp hair spread across the pillow. Derek knelt down and observed her closely. She was sound asleep, her breathing deep and even. His gaze drifted along her body, lingering over the spot where the sheet had fallen away from her breasts.

The urge to touch her was so overwhelming that it made him weak with the effort to resist. He imagined cupping the soft swell of flesh in his hand, rubbing her nipple until it grew hard. A low moan slipped from his lips and Derek sat down beside the bed, crossing his arms on the edge and studying her closely.

Who was this woman? He knew so little about her, yet he felt as if they'd known each other forever. Had they met in a different life? Or was there something deep inside them both that had drawn them together?

"Tess," he whispered.

She didn't stir. Tess. Was that short for Theresa? Or was it simply Tess? Suddenly, he had all kinds of questions he wanted to ask. He reached out and ran his fingers over her forehead, brushing the tangled hair from her eyes. She stirred, then grabbed his arm and hugged it against her, his wrist resting between her breasts.

Derek bit back another groan. There was nothing about her that had been nipped or tucked or artificially enhanced. It was rare to find a woman, especially in his social circles, who had managed to avoid the plastic surgeon. But then, Tess didn't run in the same circles as the women he'd dated.

His gaze drifted down to her leg that had slipped from beneath the bed linens. Long and slender. She obviously kept in shape riding. He could only imagine the backside that had been hidden beneath the wide skirt of her gown.

He had two choices—he could let her keep hold of his arm and lie down beside her, taking the chance that she'd respond when he touched her. Or he could be the perfect gentleman and let her sleep.

With a smile, he carefully pulled his arm out of her grasp, then stepped back, adjusting the netting above the bed. Tess Robertson would be here in the morning.

When they finally succumbed to their attraction, she wouldn't be suffering from the after-effects of too much alcohol. She'd be wide awake and clearheaded and aware of every little thing that she was experiencing with him.

He dropped the box of condoms in her bedside table, then walked to the French doors and stared out at the night sky. Up until now, he'd taken his pleasure in a woman's body without a second thought about what would come after. The future was never a consideration when it came to sex.

But for some strange reason, he wanted Tess to remember their time together. For years to come, as New Year's Eve approached, she'd remember the year she'd escaped into the night with him.

Derek raked his hand through his hair, then stepped out onto the verandah. He strolled down the stairs, knowing that it might be hours until he slept. He had so much pent-up energy that the only way to rid himself of it was to return to Tess's bed—or take matters into his own hands.

Instead, he walked up to the pool, set on a rise above the dunes. The water on the far side cascaded off the edge, creating the illusion that the pool was part of the ocean. But in the night, it was lit with soft lights, casting a wavering glow on the surrounding deck.

Derek stripped off his board shorts, his erection catching on the waistband. A soft curse slipped from his lips as he dove into the deep end. The cool water closed in over his head as he sank to the bottom, then launched himself to the surface.

With increasing speed, he swam from end to end, executing a quick flip turn and then slicing cleanly through the water. And when he was finally breathless, his muscles aching, he floated on his back into the deep end.

When he reached the side, Derek stretched his arms out along the edge of the deck and tipped his head back, the water lapping against his naked body. He rarely gave himself time to relax, but now, even if he wanted to, he couldn't think about work. His mind was completely focused on the woman he'd brought to the island.

It had always been simpler to just ignore the things lacking in his life—close friendships, hobbies, romance. All of them were impossible to have living out of a suitcase fifty weeks of the year.

Derek had always assumed he just wasn't cut out for love and commitment. After Alicia, he'd given up on serious relationships and avoided long-term entanglements. In truth, he usually knew the future of a relationship after just a few minutes together. By the time he and his date got to bed, he could predict exactly when the relationship would end.

Maybe he was just creating a reason to get out, to keep from facing the fact that he wasn't ready for something permanent. But he didn't feel that way anymore. Maybe it was genetic, programmed to kick in at a specific age. But he suddenly wanted more, something deeper, more lasting.

One thing was certain. He wasn't thinking about when his time with Tess was going to end. He was wondering how he'd make it last as long as possible.

4

THE ACHE IN HER HEAD began the moment Tess realized she was awake. Or maybe it had begun before that, she thought. Maybe that's what had woken her up. She knew it was morning, because beyond her eyelids, there was a nagging light that seemed to drill into her brain.

"Open your eyes," a voice whispered. "It'll only hurt for a second, I promise."

Tess recognized the silky warmth of Derek's tone and squinted until she could make him out. He sat on the edge of the bed, dressed only in a pair of white drawstring pants. His hair was wet, his feet were bare and he smelled like soap. But he hadn't bothered to shave.

"I have coffee and croissants, guaranteed to make you feel all better."

Tess moaned. How much had she had to drink the night before? There had been the scotch in the elevator. And then champagne on the plane. And a huge fruity punch drink on the beach…or two. She tried to recall if she'd seen Derek drinking, but she had the impression that he'd merely watched her get ploughed. "You got me drunk," she mumbled.

"You did that all on your own. And when I left you here last night, you seemed perfectly sober." He brushed the hair out of her eyes and held out a cut crystal tumbler. "Fresh orange juice. You'll feel so much better if you put something in your stomach."

Groaning, she pushed up on her elbow, then realized she was no longer wearing her party dress. In fact, she wasn't wearing anything at all! Tess peeked beneath the covers. "What happened to my clothes?"

"Don't worry, I didn't look," he said. "At least not for long."

"How did I—" A memory flashed in her mind. "Oh, right." She'd undressed herself. They'd come back to her room. After he'd left, she'd stripped off her wet clothes and crawled right into bed…ready to plunge ahead with a full-scale seduction. She hadn't been drunk. But she must have been so exhausted she'd fallen asleep the moment she hit the sheets.

"There's sand in my bed," she murmured, wincing at the uncomfortable feeling.

"Don't worry. The housekeeping staff will come and change the sheets." He leaned over and stole a kiss. "You know what really helps a hangover?" he asked. "Another drink. I can send out for mimosas."

"Oh, I never want to drink again," she said, pulling the pillow over her face. Her hands tangled in her hair—hair that had been wet when she fell asleep. Tess groaned again. She probably looked as bad as she felt. "Do you think you could leave me alone and let me deal with this on my own?"

He reached out and smoothed his hand along her bare arm. "I think you look beautiful." A tiny thrill shot through her and she pulled the pillow away to look at him. Oh, God, he was even sexier in the light of day. "You are such a good liar," she said.

"Come on," he said. "Take a shower and we'll have breakfast together." He wove his fingers through hers and gently pulled her out of bed. She grabbed the sheet, tugging it around her naked body. She was sure he'd already seen what she was trying to hide, but Tess had at least a few inhibitions left.

She raked her fingers through her hair. "Shower," she murmured.

"Kiss first," he said.

"Just one," Tess said. He caught her around the waist and touched his lips to hers in a sweet and tempting kiss. Then he handed her the orange juice. Tess took a sip and smiled. "Oh, that does taste good."

Derek pointed to a pile of clothes. "I raided Chloe's closet. Some of the things still have tags."

Tess picked through the colorful assortment of bikinis, sarongs and cotton sundresses. He'd even brought along a wide-brimmed straw hat and a pair of sunglasses. She noticed there was no underwear. "These are nice," she said, turning to face him.

"I'll leave you," Derek said.

"You can stay. I'll only be a few minutes."

"If I stay, we're going to end up in the shower together. Then in your bed. And that will probably go on for the rest of the day. So I think I'll give you a little time to recover first."

She stared at him, a bit shocked by his admission, yet pleased at the same time. Her breathing suddenly became quick and shallow. "Okay," Tess said in a strangled tone.

Derek grinned, then gave her another quick kiss. "Follow the beach path to the left and go up the steps. The pool is on the other side of the house."

Tess managed a smile and watched as he strode to the door. When he was gone, she pressed a hand to her forehead and let out a tightly held breath. The pounding in her head wasn't nearly as bad as it had been lying down. And the blood rushing through her body was doing a great deal to restore her energy. A shared shower was an intriguing possibility. She'd never showered with a man before.

Slowly, Tess crossed the room and examined the breakfast Derek had left behind. A croissant was just the thing to settle her roiling stomach and the thick, dark coffee would wake her up. He'd even brought a bottle of aspirin. A gardenia on the breakfast tray filled the room with an exotic scent and she tucked it behind her ear and stared at her reflection in the mirror on the wall.

"Hello." Tess had looked at herself in the mirror thousands of times, but she'd never closely examined her appearance. As she studied her reflection now, she barely recognized the woman staring back at her. Her cheeks were flushed and her eyes bright and her hair tumbled around her face. She looked…sexy.

A tiny smile twitched at the corners of her mouth. Was this the woman Derek was so attracted to? What did he see in her that she'd never noticed in herself? All her makeup had been washed away the night before and her face was bare and rather plain, yet he'd just told her she was beautiful.

She ran her hands over her cheeks. "I look…healthy," she murmured with a shrug. Not skinny, not curvaceous, but somewhere in between. "Maybe he has a thing for healthy women."

Tess wandered into the bathroom and turned on the shower. She set the gardenia next to the sink before stepping beneath the cascade of water. As she closed her eyes, an image of Derek drifted through her mind.

What might have happened last night had she not fallen asleep? Would they have made love? Would they have been sharing this shower? Sighing softly, she turned her face up into the spray and ran her hands over her naked skin.

Every nerve of her body seemed at attention and ready to react. She felt as if surrender was just a matter of a simple caress or a long, probing kiss. Though waiting was delicious torture, Tess wondered whether she'd be able to live up to his expectations.

He'd obviously had a good deal of experience with women. A guy like Derek would have had his choice of sexual partners—models, actresses, celebrities. There wasn't a single guy on the planet that would turn a beautiful woman away when presented with the opportunity.

Though Tess was aware of the full range of adult sexual activities, she hadn't enjoyed a wide practical knowledge. Sex with Jeffrey had been rather uninspiring. She could count the number of lovers she'd had on one hand. And none of them had been particularly adventurous in the bedroom. Would her relative inexperience show the moment she and Derek began? Or could she fake her way through this?

By the time she emerged from the shower, Tess was feeling more like herself, but her insecurities nagged at her confidence. There was nothing to be ashamed of, she thought to herself. It was who she was. Healthy and slightly inexperienced. But that didn't mean she was ready to become someone else once they got busy.

She wrapped a thick terrycloth robe around her wet body, tucked the gardenia behind her ear, then sat down at the table and continued with her breakfast. Desire was a strange thing. Already, she felt different, more aware and alive than she'd ever been before.

When she finished her second croissant, Tess gulped down another glass of juice and then poured herself a cup of coffee. Renewed and revived, she let her robe drop to the floor, then picked up a bright blue bikini that Derek had provided, examining it carefully.

She hadn't put on a swim suit since she was a teenager. The bottom piece had a thong back and the top was no more than two tiny triangles held together by a few strings. She held it up in front of her naked body, staring into the mirror. Her backside had always been her best feature, toned by lots of riding and usually hidden beneath a pair of faded jeans.

"Well, at least I'll be putting all my best assets out there," she said, tugging the thong up over her hips.

"I think you'll look great in that."

Tess looked up to find Derek watching her from the doorway. She quickly covered her breasts with her arms, then realized that there was no reason to hide herself from him. A girl with experience would let him look.

His gaze slowly drifted down her body and she stood rooted to the spot, enjoying the attention. "I might as well go naked," she said, her heart slamming in her chest as she dropped her arms.

Derek nodded. "I have no objection to that."

Emboldened, she untangled the top, then slipped it over her head. Turning to her back to him, Tess glanced over her shoulder. "Can you tie that?"

He crossed the room. She felt his fingers fumble with the strings, brushing up against her bare back. He cursed softly and then, with a sigh, finally managed a tight knot. His palms smoothed across her shoulders and down her arms, then slipped around her waist.

"Let's go get some sun," he whispered.

Tess grabbed the sunglasses and straw hat from the dresser. Derek walked to the door and waited for her. But before she could step outside, he grabbed her hand and spun her around to face him. His hands cupped her face as he pulled her into a long, desperate kiss.

"Forget the sun," he murmured. "It'll still be there when we're finished."

It was as simple as that, she thought. No nervous conversations or tentative caresses. Just pure, raw need. His hands were all over her, from her shoulders to her breasts to her hips and back again. He moved against her and before long, he was hard and ready beneath the thin fabric of the pants he wore.

The instinct to connect, to test the limits of their desires was undeniable. Tess dropped the hat and the sunglasses on the floor, then turned in his arms. She placed her palm on his chest, smoothing it over deeply tanned skin and hard muscle. Her pulse quickened as she leaned forward and pressed a kiss to his nipple, softly teasing at it with her tongue before moving to the other.

Tess had never been so uninhibited, but it seemed easy to toss aside her fears. There were no hidden agendas, no hopes for a future between them. Everything they wanted was here for the taking. So why not enjoy?

An instant later, his fingers tangled in her hair and he tipped her face up to meet his lips. As the kiss deepened, Tess realized she'd never experienced this kind pleasure with another man. Her body craved his touch and ached for a deeper contact.

Taking her hand, Derek pulled her along to the bed, their lips still tasting, tongues still teasing. They fell into the rumpled bed linens, Derek yanking her down on top of him. He pulled the bikini top over her head and tossed it aside then trailed a line of kisses along the curve of her neck. When he reached her breast, he circled her nipple with his tongue then gently drew it into his mouth.

The pleasure was too much to bear and Tess cried out, holding him close as desire pulsed through her body.

"I've been thinking about doing this all night long," he murmured.

"Why didn't you stay with me last night?"

"Because, when it finally happened between us, I wanted both of us to remember it." He smiled as he rolled her onto her back, then moved to her other breast. Her fingers furrowed through his damp hair and he molded his mouth to her flesh. "Will you remember it now?" he whispered.

"Yes," she replied, breathless. "Oh, yes."

"And you won't have any regrets later?"

Tess shook her head. "No. Why would I regret this?"

"Until I kidnapped you, you were on your way to getting engaged."

"Don't worry about that," she said.

In truth, since Alison's call last night, Tess had put Jeffrey out of her mind for good. That should tell her something about her feelings for the man, shouldn't it? She was relieved it was over, relieved she didn't have to give him an answer to the question she thought he was planning to ask.

"How much longer do we have to wait to take the rest of our clothes off?" she asked.

"Now would be fine," he replied.

It was so comfortable, being with Derek, Tess thought. She had no hang-ups, no insecurities. She could be herself, or maybe a better version of herself. With a giggle, she crawled off the bed and stood in front of him. Slowly, she shimmied out of the bikini bottoms.

Derek sat up, bracing his hands behind him. "God, you are so beautiful. Just perfect."

Tess had never believed she was anything out of the ordinary. But now, with Derek looking at her, his eyes glazed with desire, she could believe it. Tess crawled over him on the bed and untied the drawstring at his waist, then slowly pulled the loose cotton pants down.

His smooth shaft was hard and ready. The moment she tossed his pants on the floor, he slipped his hand around her waist and pulled their naked bodies together. His cock pressed against her stomach, the hard ridge meeting soft flesh. And when she reached down to caress him, Tess heard him suck in a sharp breath and then groan softly as her fingers closed around him.

NOTHING HAD PREPARED Derek for the intensity of his need. Last night had been just one long tease and when it was over, he had been resigned to sleeping alone. But now he realized the anticipation had only made this moment more incredible. They were both completely clearheaded and wide awake and caught in a riptide of desire.

He ran his hands over her naked body as she caressed him, her flesh warm and soft against his palms. Already it was taking more willpower than he had to maintain control. He wanted to bury himself inside her, to feel her warmth surround him.

But Derek fought the urge to rush. Every moment that they shared was a chance to know her better, to find out what fired her desire. Though they were almost strangers, there was an undeniable connection between them, as if they'd known each other for weeks and months instead of just hours.

Derek drew her beneath him, then slowly began a careful exploration of her body. She arched as he moved down from her breast to her belly and then to a spot just above her hip. Everything about her aroused him, from the scent of her skin to the tiny beauty mark he discovered on her thigh.

Was there anything about her that he didn't find fascinating? Derek tried to remember the last time he'd wanted a woman as much as he wanted Tess, but the effort to even recall his past lovers didn't seem worth the time. This woman was…everything.

Derek slid off the bed and gently kissed the insides of her thighs. He moved higher and when he found the damp spot between her legs, he flicked his tongue along the crease. Her body jerked in response, but he couldn't stop there. Gently, he began to tease her, waiting for each response and then using it to his advantage.

Her fingers clutched at his hair, pulling him forward and then pushing him away when the sensations became too much for her to bear. Derek sensed when she'd reached her limit but didn't want to stop. How far could he take her? He wanted her to surrender and yet he wanted to experience that delicious capitulation along with her.

He stretched out on the bed and nuzzled her neck, gently keeping her on the edge with his fingers. Tess stared at him through passion-glazed eyes. "I knew this would be good," she whispered.

Derek growled softly. "And we've only just started."

She nodded, her lower lip caught between teeth. "I'm not sure I'll be very good at this."

"Don't worry. We have lots of time to practice."

She wrapped her arm around his head and pulled him close. "I'm a very dedicated student." Her breath caught in her throat and she moaned softly.

Her body writhed beneath his touch and she reached out to wrap her fingers around his shaft. The moment she touched him, Derek realized that sleeping in separate beds the night before had done nothing to diminish his craving for release. Every nerve in his body felt like it was on fire. He reached over and grabbed the box of condoms he'd tossed on her bedside table.

"Did you bring those with breakfast?" she asked.

He handed her the package. "Last night. I thought there might be a chance this would happen. And then I found you asleep."

"I'm not asleep now." Tess took the box from him and tore open a package. As she sheathed him, Derek realized how close he was to the end of it all. Suddenly, he wanted to delay, to stop this headlong race toward satisfaction. How long would they have together? Would he be flying her back home before nightfall? He sighed softly as he settled between her legs.

"Stay with me," he whispered. "Promise that we'll have more than just this. Until tomorrow."

"I promise," she murmured.

He waited to enter her, marshalling his self-control and focusing on something other than her naked body.

"What's wrong?" Tess asked.

"I'm kind of nervous," he said.

She wrapped her arms around his neck and laughed. "Why?"

Derek nuzzled his face into her neck. "I'm usually really good at this," he said. "Really. I can give you references. But I want this to be better than I've ever imagined it could be."

"I don't need references," she said. "I prefer to formulate my own opinions."

"And what is your opinion so far?" He probed gently at her entrance, then slipped inside of her. The breath left his body. He moved slowly, burying himself inch by inch. He was good at this, Derek thought to himself. That was one thing he was sure of. When he was buried completely, he waited, knowing that it would take every ounce of his control to hold back and wait for her.

"I—I think you're doing—just fine," she replied with tiny gasps.

He moved, drawing back and then plunging a little deeper. Every thrust brought a new pinnacle of pleasure. He read her responses, her soft sighs and breathless pleas, the way her body reacted to their joining. And when she finally dissolved into uncontrollable spasms, it was all he could do to hold on for just a few more minutes. He became lost in a maelstrom of incredible sensation.

She was everything he'd hoped she'd be—passionate, uninhibited, responsive. With every kiss and every thrust, he felt as if they'd discovered something beautiful to share. This was totally new to him. The physical connection was undeniable, but there was something deeper at work. He just couldn't put words to it.

As the passion grew more intense between them, self-awareness vanished and instinct took over. He focused only on the pleasure that each movement brought.

Grabbing her waist, he pulled her on top of him, anxious to watch her reaction to what they were experiencing. Tess's hair fell in unruly waves around her flushed face. Derek reached up and smoothed the strands back and she met his gaze. A lazy smile touched her lips and he had all the answers he needed.

When he reached between them and touched her, the contact startled her for a moment. And then she moaned softly and slowed her pace. Slowly, his caress transformed her, bringing Tess closer and closer to the edge. He'd never really paid attention to the pleasure he gave a woman. But now, as he watched her surrender to her own need, Derek recognized the emotional connection that could come along with sex.

She was completely vulnerable, trusting him to provide what she sought. And when Tess cried out and spasms shook her body, he knew this wasn't just about physical satisfaction. They'd shared something deeper and more intense, something that now bound them together. With one last thrust, he joined her, gripping her hips as his orgasm overwhelmed him.

After it was over, they lay side-by-side, limbs still entwined, heartbeats growing slower. Derek pressed his forehead to hers, searching for the words to express how he felt. But his brain was a muddle of contradictory thoughts. He felt exhilarated but sober, confused yet clearheaded, content yet strangely unsatisfied.

"I think you completely cured my hangover," she murmured. "I feel much better."

"It's all that blood pumping through your body," he said. "Orgasms are good for you. Very healthy."

"Good to know," Tess said. "Next time I catch a cold, I'll have to give you a call."

Derek pulled her leg over his hip, drawing her closer. "I'd be happy to help."

Her naked body fit so perfectly against his, as if she were made especially for him. Derek brushed the thought aside. It would be stupid to make something out of this that wasn't really there. Hell, Tess still had a boyfriend back at home, a guy she'd intended to marry until he came along. And even though she'd decided to give infidelity a try, he was still the "other" man.

"Why did you come with me?" Derek asked. "When we got out of the elevator, why didn't you go upstairs to your party?"

Tess sighed softly, then shrugged. "I don't know. I never do things like this. I'm not an impetuous person.

Every decision I make, I think about for days and days before I finally decide. But with you…it just seemed like the right thing to do." She paused. "It's almost like you'd come to rescue me." She reached up and smoothed her fingertips along his lower lip. "Why did you ask me to come with you?"

"You looked like you needed rescuing. And you were so beautiful, all dressed up in that gown. I liked the way you spoke to me. You weren't trying to flirt or play games. You were direct and honest. And you drank scotch right out of the bottle."

"Maybe I've gone a little crazy. But I'm glad I came with you and—" Tess's phone rang, the funny melody filling the room and breaking the mood that had enveloped them. "I can guess who that is," she said.

"Your boyfriend?"

Tess shook her head. "Alison. I'll just let it ring. I can call her back later."

Derek pushed up and reached over Tess, grabbing the phone from the bedside table. He flipped it open and handed it to her. "Tell her you're safe."

"Hello?" she said.

He listened to her side of the conversation, trying to discern her true feelings about what they'd shared in the things she revealed to Alison. After only a few minutes, she handed the phone to him. "She wants to talk to you," Tess said.

Derek took the phone. "Hi, Alison. We're having a wonderful time. Wish you were here."

"All right. From what I can tell, you've been a gentleman, so I'm going to take it easy on you. But I want you to know that Tess has put up with enough crap in her life already. She doesn't deserve to be trifled with."

"Trifled?" Derek asked. "What does that word even mean?"

"Don't get impertinent with me. You know what I'm saying. Don't make promises you can't keep. Don't lead her to believe you feel something you don't. And when she wants to come home, let her go."

"All right," Derek said. "I can do that."

"Good. Now, go back to whatever you were doing and have a nice day."

The line went dead and Derek handed the phone to Tess. "She's really a ball buster," he murmured.

"She worries about me," Tess explained. "We worry about each other. We're best friends."

"She wants us to go back to what we were doing. Do you think she realized we were lying in your bed, naked?"

"Probably not."

"If she knew, she might just fly down here and cut off my…what did she call them?"

"Manparts. And I think she's concerned that I might fall in love," Tess said. "But she doesn't have to worry. There will be no more falling in love for me."

What was that supposed to mean? Had she fallen in love for the last time with this Jeffrey guy she intended to marry? Damn it, he knew this was nothing more than a fling and yet he continually allowed himself to believe it was something more. It wasn't that easy to turn off his feelings when it came to this woman.

"Right," he murmured. "No falling in love here either."

TESS CLOSED HER EYES and tipped her face up to the sun. A fresh breeze blew off the water, smelling of the Caribbean. This was paradise. All of her anxieties and concerns seemed so far away, blown offshore by the wind to a place where they couldn't bother her.

Funny how things had changed so quickly. Just yesterday, she was getting ready for the party, her mind filled with thoughts of a future with Jeffrey. Unbidden, a wave of anger surged inside of her, but she pushed it back. Jeffrey Beale had done her a favor. Deep down, in her heart of hearts, she'd sensed the relationship would never have worked. She just hadn't been able to admit it to herself.

How could she have been fooled so completely? He'd never loved her. He'd only been using her as a...distraction. Sleeping with the help. It was a story as old as time itself. Part of her wanted to confront him about his duplicity, to throw it back in his face. Had he purposely invited her to the party to humiliate her in front of all of his parents' wealthy friends? Or was he trying to send a message, telling her she could never exist in his world? That is, if he'd sent the invitation at all...

At least with Derek, she knew exactly where she stood. There'd be no thoughts of a future with him. What they shared was strictly rooted in the present. And there wouldn't be enough time for dishonesty.

Tess turned her head and looked at him. He lay beside her on the chaise, his chest already turning a deeper brown in the intense sun. He was so incredibly beautiful. She'd never imagined having such a lover.

A tiny thrill raced though her. She had a lover. That sounded so worldly, so sophisticated. And so *not* her! But Tess had come to appreciate the benefits of casual sex. She'd never experienced such a powerful connection with a man, never allowed herself to completely surrender. With Derek, it was easy to fall into the fantasy, to step outside herself and respond fully to his touch.

She rolled to her side and reached out, tracing a line down the center of his chest, following a soft trail of hair that disappeared below his waistband. They'd explored each other's bodies that morning and she knew what his clothes hid. There was a secret pleasure in that.

His eyes still closed, Derek caught her fingers, then brought them up to his lips. "You're interrupting my nap," he complained.

"Only old men take naps," she said. "How old are you?"

"Old enough. And men who've been sexually exhausted by beautiful but insatiable women need their rest," he said. "So cut me a break, will you?"

"Insatiable?" she asked. "I was very satiable. I was satiable three times this morning."

"Three?" He rolled to his side and faced her, his gaze skimming her face. "I thought it was only two."

"Once the first time and twice the second."

"Hmm, I missed one then."

"You were kind of busy yourself," she said, reaching out to brush his hair out of his eyes. She sighed softly and turned her face back up to the sun. "Is there anything better than this? If there is, I've never experienced it."

"I don't think so," Derek said. "There's nothing more in this world that I could possibly want."

"Me neither," she said.

He smoothed his hand from her waist up to her breast, gently rubbing his thumb across her nipple. She'd decided to go topless at Derek's insistence. "You're getting sunburned," he said. "You need to put on more lotion or cover up."

Tess sat up and grabbed the bottle from the end of the chaise and handed it to him. "Do my back, will you?" She pulled her hair to the side and smiled as Derek rubbed suntan lotion across her shoulders. "Just the smell of this lotion makes me relax." She turned and grabbed the bottle from him, taking a deep whiff. "I'd like to take this bottle home with me. Whenever I need to relax, I'll just take a whiff."

"Why is it you've never had a real vacation?" he asked, gently massaging her shoulders.

"Horses require constant care," she said. "You just can't turn the chores over to the neighbors for a week or two. And the last thing you want is for the owners to think they can do without you. There's always someone waiting just outside the gate, ready to convince the owners that they can do it better and cheaper."

He rested his chin on her shoulder. "So, what do you think will happen when you're gone this weekend?" Derek asked.

"Nothing," she said. "I have a really good staff at the farm. And I was planning to stay in Nashville until Monday anyway. Today is Friday."

"You were supposed to be spending the New Year's weekend with your fiancé?"

She nodded. "I assumed that was the plan. Until I met you."

"How are you going to explain this to him?" Derek asked.

"I won't have to," Tess said. "It's not important anymore." She wanted to tell him about Jeffrey's duplicity, but she couldn't bring herself to admit her own stupidity. It was far better to have him think she'd run away from an engagement and was carrying on an illicit affair with him, than to know the truth. It made her seem much more mysterious.

"Three days," Derek murmured. "We could get into a lot of trouble in three days."

"Promise?" She turned around on the chaise and faced him, tucking her knees under her chin. "I'm willing to get into all kinds of trouble," Tess said. "But you need to know that I don't have any expectations. Only that we'll have a really good time together and then we'll go our separate ways."

"That's it?"

"This is just a fantasy, Derek. It's not supposed to be real. I know that. I don't need anything more." She looked into his eyes, hoping to read his reaction, but couldn't. "We're agreed then?"

"Of course," Derek said. "This will be strictly NSA."

"NSA?"

"No strings attached," he said. He smiled as he reached out and began to rub lotion on her hip. "Speaking of strings." Derek hooked his finger beneath the string that held up her bikini bottom. "It would be a shame if you got tan lines. Maybe you need to get rid of these strings, too."

"Then I would be completely naked," Tess said.

"I know," he replied. "That's what I was thinking." He leaned forward and dropped a kiss on her lips. "Come on. You're on vacation. Live dangerously."

"You want me to live dangerously?" she asked, rising to his challenge. She'd always wanted to be dangerous. "What about you? You still have your shorts on."

"I could take those off. Then we'd both be naked."

"I dare you. If you take your shorts off, I'll take my bottoms off." She lay back on the chaise and stretched her hands over her head. "I think I'm going to need more lotion on my front, please. I wouldn't want to get a sunburn."

He groaned softly. "I see what you mean." Derek squirted lotion into his palm and slowly began to rub it over her right breast.

"Oh, that feels so good," she moaned. "You do that so well. Don't stop."

"Stop teasing," he warned.

"No, really. Do the other one." She wriggled beneath his touch, taunting him until he finally gave in and crawled on top of her, catching her mouth in a long, delicious kiss.

"All right, maybe complete nudity isn't the best idea. You've made your point."

"No, no," Tess continued. "I like living dangerously. If you take your shorts off, I'll rub lotion all over you." She grabbed the lotion and reached for the waistband of his shorts.

Derek hopped to his feet and pulled her up along with him. "I think we should go for a walk," he said. "Come on." He grabbed a towel and draped it over her shoulders, covering her bare breasts. "I need to take my mind off your rather intriguing body parts."

"Why?"

"Because, if I don't occasionally do that, we'd be spending all our time in bed."

"I wonder if that's what a honeymoon is like?" Tess asked.

"Probably. Except, if this were a honeymoon, I'd get to keep you when it was all over."

She slipped her arm around his waist as he pulled her against him. "You would definitely not want to keep me. I can be a real pain in the ass."

They walked out to the beach and stood silently on the sand, staring out at the turquoise water. The beach was small and private, secluded from the resort beach by a rocky area filled with a tangle of scrub and undergrowth. Their chaise from the night before was still there, sitting beneath a colorful beach umbrella.

Tess walked to the edge of the water, dropped her towel, and ran into the surf. Grabbing a breath, she dove beneath the surface, then bobbed up, pushing her hair out of her eyes.

A few moments later, he was beside her, holding on to her waist as the surging water pushed them closer to the shore. "Kiss me," he murmured, water dripping from his wet hair, his lashes sparkling with tiny droplets.

Tess wrapped her arms around his neck and did as he asked. How simple it was to please him, she mused, her body sliding against his provocatively. She leaned back, spreading her arms and floating on the surface as he held her.

This was all so unfamiliar to her, yet she felt perfectly at ease in his world. Maybe this was all she needed to change the course of her life. She'd been so thoroughly stuck in a rut for years, worrying about her father and their finances. It felt wonderful to cast all that aside for a few days and just exist.

"What do you want?" he asked. "I'll give you anything you want."

"I want to swim naked with you," she said, her mind floating as lazily as her body.

"You're not wearing much as it is," Derek said.

"But you are." Tess pulled herself out of the water, clinging to his neck as she pressed a kiss on his salt-flavored lips. "Take off your shorts."

"But what if I get all aroused?" he teased, mocking her earlier concerns.

Tess slipped out of her bikini bottoms and then hurled them toward the shore. They landed in a few feet of water, floating on the surface. Derek did the same, but his throw landed on top of her towel.

As they stood in waist-deep water, his hands smoothed over the curves of her slick skin, creating a whole new sensation of intimacy. His lips followed his hands, gently kissing and sucking. Tess took the time for her own exploration, caught up in the sheer masculine beauty of his form, the sun-burnished skin, the hard muscles of his chest, and the chiseled features of his face.

Someday, when she was back in the real world, lying alone in her bed, she'd remember this moment. She felt as if he'd uncovered her soul. She'd been transformed into a woman who reveled in the pleasures of the flesh, who knew her power over a man's body. A woman who was just discovering the depths of her own passion.

"I don't know who I am anymore," Tess murmured.

He drew back, twisting his fingers in her wet hair and tipping her head back until she met his gaze. "I'm starting to realize that I don't either."

"Aren't we a pair," she said.

His eyes fixed on her mouth. "At least we have that in common." His lips came down on hers in a long, languid kiss. She felt giddy and light-headed, unable to think about anything but the sensations racing through her body. This was paradise. And Tess wasn't sure she ever wanted to leave.

5

TESS AND DEREK STOOD in the kitchen, staring into the huge refrigerator and silently studying the contents. "I could make you a sandwich," he suggested. "Or we could just order something from the resort."

He stepped away and watched as Tess picked through the meager supplies, his gaze dropping to her backside. For a woman who'd come to the island with a lot of baggage, she'd managed to discard it pretty quickly. She was wearing just her bikini thong, her bare breasts exposed as if she had spent her entire life half-naked.

Derek jumped up to sit on the edge of the counter, waiting for her to turn around, so he might enjoy the front view as well.

"Could we go to the grocery store?" she asked, examining an apple she'd found.

"That would require a boat ride," he said. Derek pulled out a drawer beneath his legs and found a piece of paper and a pen. "Here, write down what you want and I'll have it sent from the resort. They'll make you anything you want, a sandwich or a gourmet meal." He leaned back, bracing his arms behind him.

She began to scribble a list, then looked up to find him staring at her. "What? Do you want to make the list?"

Derek shook his head, then reached out and slowly toyed with the strings on her bikini bottom. "Nope. I'm just taking in the view." He arched his eyebrow as he saw her cheeks flush. "You seem to be pretty comfortable with the dress code around here."

"I'm getting used to it," she said, a sly smile on her lips. "Although I've never been so bold before."

Derek grabbed her waist and pulled her between his legs. He cupped her breast with his palm, slowly stroking her nipple until it grew taut and hard. "Why hide a body like this?"

"We are alone, aren't we?" she asked. "No one will walk in on us?"

"Nope," he said. "The only other people on the island are at the resort. They don't come to the house unless we call them."

"And where is this resort you're always talking about?"

"It's down on the other end of the island," he said. "It's very private—that's why a lot of celebrities come here. There are ten bungalows and a restaurant and pool. Each of the bungalows has a private beach. And we have boats. We keep our sailboat over there," he said, pointing towards a small marina. "We can have lunch over at the restaurant and I'll show you around."

Tess glanced down at his lap, then smoothed her hand over the crotch of his shorts. He was already growing hard, simply from touching her. "We could do that," she murmured, slipping her fingers beneath the waistband. "Maybe a little later."

As she continued to caress him, Derek lost himself in the wild sensations coursing through his body. She tugged at the shorts, pulling them down over his hips and freeing him from the damp fabric.

Derek raked his hand through her hair, pulling it away from her face. "Yeah, I guess lunch can wait."

He knew exactly what was coming but was unprepared for the effect that it would have on him. When her lips closed around him, he sucked in a sharp breath, then slowly let it out. A tremor raced through his body and a groan slipped from his throat. Though the feeling of burying himself inside her body was something he craved, this came in a close second.

Every moment they spent together revealed a new discovery. Her mouth was warm and wet and with each stroke, he fought the orgasm that threatened to end it all. Watching her made that task nearly impossible.

Derek closed his eyes and tipped his head back, but that didn't help at all. It only gave him the chance to focus more intently on what she was doing to him. It wasn't like he'd never experienced this before. But in the past, indulging gave him nothing more than momentary pleasure and physical relief. This was so much more.

They'd each surrendered, each exposed their vulnerabilities, and with that came a trust he'd never shared with another woman. He didn't have to hide from Tess. He could share anything with her, do anything with her, and there would be no regrets.

When he came close again, Derek sat up and took her face between his hands, drawing her up to indulge in a long, deep kiss. She continued to stroke him with her hand and he lasted only a few minutes longer before his control dissolved beneath her fingers.

When the waves of need finally subsided, she looked up at him and smiled. "In the kitchen," she murmured. "We are naughty."

"We are," he said.

She ran her palm along his shaft. "I like it."

He kissed her again, his fingers furrowing through her hair and molding her mouth to his. "We need to finish your list," he said. "Unless you want me to return the favor?"

She shook her head. "I can wait. Right now, I'm hungry for food."

He stood behind her as she wrote, adding items as they came to mind. In truth, he was glad they'd be cooking for themselves. She enjoyed their isolation far more than he'd ever anticipated.

The kitchen phone rang and Derek ignored it, knowing it was probably a member of his family.

"Shouldn't you answer that?" Tess asked.

He shook his head and grabbed the pen, adding his favorite beer to the list. "No. I'm hungry, too, and I want to get something to eat." He draped his arm around her shoulder and toyed with her hair. "It's probably just my mother. I'm sure Chloe told her I'm here. I don't need to talk to her now."

"What if someone's calling to say they're coming down here?"

Derek understood her concern. He didn't want to be interrupted either. Impatiently, he picked up the phone. "Hello?"

"It's about time!" He recognized Chloe's voice. "I've been calling your cell phone for the last two hours."

"We've been…busy," Derek said. "What do you want?"

"I just talked to Mom and she had some really startling news and I thought you might want to know."

"Chloe, I don't—"

"Alicia has left Sam. It happened right after Christmas. She says the marriage is over. She wants a divorce."

The news left him speechless for a moment. And then he realized he felt nothing—for either his brother or his former fiancée. "So? Both you and I knew their marriage was a mistake from the start. Are you surprised?"

"That's not why I'm calling. Sam thought she might be coming down to the island. I just wanted to warn you."

Derek cursed softly. "She can't get here unless she comes in on a plane or a boat. And she won't be using any of ours. If she does show up, I'll just tell her to leave."

"Mom thought she might be looking for you. I guess your name came up in their last argument."

"Great," he muttered. "I really need to jump back into the middle of this right now."

"Well, I wasn't sure how you'd feel. That's why I called."

"Are you asking if I care? No, Chloe. That whole thing is over. Done. Finished. Get a message to Alicia or Sam or Mom and tell them she's not welcome here."

"Oh, I'd love to do that for you," Chloe said with a wicked giggle. "Say hello to Tess for me."

"I will," he said. He hung up the phone then glanced at Tess, who was watching him with a curious gaze. "It's nothing. Chloe says hello."

"Why was she calling? Is she coming back?"

Derek shook his head. "No."

"Is someone else coming?"

"No."

"You look worried."

"I'm not," he said, forcing a smile. Derek reached out and rubbed her arm, but it didn't erase the concern etching her brow.

She opened her mouth, then snapped it shut. "I'm going back to the pool." Tess opened the fridge and grabbed a bottle of water and the apple she'd found earlier. "You know, the thing I like best about you is that you're honest. But I get the feeling you're not being honest with me right now."

"Tess, come on. It's nothing, I swear. It's just some family stuff, that's all."

"Fine," she said.

She walked to the door and Derek watched her leave, the sight of her backside enough to make him groan with frustration. She was right. There was no reason not to tell her about Sam and Alicia—beyond the fact that it made him look like a sap for falling in love with Alicia in the first place.

And they had been open and honest with each other until now. Maybe she was right. Maybe that's what made this relationship so perfect. They weren't keeping secrets. But if he told her, he'd have to explain the whole sordid mess.

Determined to set things right, Derek called the resort to order their groceries, then headed out to the pool to find Tess. She was floating in a pool chair when he got there. She'd put her top back on and wore the huge sunhat he'd given her along with a pair of sunglasses.

"You're right," he called. "We should be completely honest with each other."

"Absolutely," she said.

"Will you come here? I need to tell you something."

"I'm listening," she said, her hands lazily creating ripples as she moved toward him.

Derek sat down at the edge of the pool, his legs dangling in the water. "The first thing you need to know is that I don't love her anymore. I'm not sure when I stopped, but it's completely over between us. It has been for a long time."

"This isn't beginning well," Tess said. "Who are you talking about?"

"Alicia. My former fiancée."

She took off her sunglasses and looked at him. "You were engaged?"

"Five years ago. I thought I loved her. I was stupid and she was looking to get ahead. She was an interior designer in our corporate offices and I thought I was ready for marriage."

"What happened?"

"I found her in bed with my older brother, Sam. And then, as if that wasn't humiliation enough, *they* decided to get married. Our once pleasant family holidays turned into a giant, seething soap opera."

"I'm sorry," she said. "That must have been terrible."

"It was. But you know the really awful thing? My parents just expected me to accept what had happened and be happy for the two of them. Like everything I'd invested in my future with her didn't make a difference. Don't you find that odd?"

"Maybe they were just trying to keep peace," she suggested.

"Or maybe the fact that they were grooming Sam to take over the business colored their reaction. No scandals for him. Everything was very hush-hush."

"Why was your sister calling?" she asked.

He held out his hand and crooked his finger in her direction. "I'd feel much better about telling you all this if you'd come over here and kiss me."

She slipped off the chair and walked to the side of the pool. Pushing up on her toes, she brushed a kiss across his lips. "Why was your sister calling?"

"She thought Alicia might be coming down here. She and Sam just split up and she took off. She's always liked this place."

"Is she coming here for you?"

"She doesn't know I'm here." He frowned. "Unless she called the resort and they told her." Derek shook his head. "Don't worry, she's not going to interrupt us. If she comes, we'll leave."

He pushed off the edge of the pool and dropped into the water. His hands smoothed over her body and they indulged in a long, lazy kiss as the water closed in around them.

He didn't love Alicia. Though he'd carried a rather big torch around long after she'd dumped him, that torch had burned out. Derek tried to remember when he'd stopped feeling burned by what had happened, but it didn't really matter. He had Tess and she'd erased every other woman from his mind.

"I'm not going to let anyone or anything ruin this fantasy," he murmured, pressing a line of kisses along her shoulder. "Alicia is old news."

"I understand, you know," she said. "How it feels. Like someone just punched you in the stomach. Like everything you thought was true was just a figment of your imagination."

"Exactly."

She wrapped her arms around his neck, pressing her lips to his chest. "It happened to me, too."

"How long has it been?" Derek asked.

"Less than twenty-four hours," Tess replied.

He took a step back, shocked by her admission. "What are you talking about?"

"Remember last night when I had that meltdown? I checked my phone and there was a text message on it from Alison. Jeffrey announced his engagement at the party. Only it wasn't to me."

Derek gasped. "How is that possible? I thought you were…weren't you…I don't understand. Why would he do that?"

"What I believed to be a serious relationship was just a seedy affair. He was obviously sleeping with me whenever he came to the farm and romancing some debutante when he wasn't. Talk about a soap opera."

Though he felt bad for Tess, he couldn't help but be encouraged by the news. They were both completely free to pursue their relationship. "I'm sorry. That must have been…"

"Slightly humiliating," she said. "Even from hundreds of miles away. But at least I wasn't at the party when he made the announcement. That would have been mortifying." Tess smiled up at him. "You saved me from that. You and the broken elevator."

"We are a pair, aren't we?"

Tess laughed and pushed away from him, kicking to the other side of the pool and splashing water in his face. Derek dove beneath the water and popped up in front of her, then pulled her down.

She came up sputtering, then splashed him. "You're lucky I like you."

"Why do you like me?" he challenged.

She leaned forward and dropped a kiss on his lips. "I like you because you have a jet." Her expression dissolved into teasing laughter and Derek grabbed her by the waist and dragged her to the center of the pool.

"Why do you like me?" he asked again, threatening to dunk her once more.

"Because—because you're a fantastic lover!" she cried.

He set her back on her feet. "Is that all?" Derek asked softly.

"No," she said. "Do you really want the truth?"

"Absolutely."

"I like you because you like me the way I am. And that makes me feel…good. Happy."

Derek was caught off guard by her words. In truth, he felt the same way about Tess. They seemed to understand each other without really having to explain themselves. Why was that? They were little more than strangers who had shared a bed and yet it felt as if he'd known her all his life. He bent close and kissed her, a soft, sweet kiss that seemed to go on forever. "I want you to feel safe with me."

There were moments when he wondered at the circumstances that brought them together. He could have taken the next elevator. She could have gone to her party and been humiliated by the man she'd loved. And this perfect fantasy would have never happened.

"I think we need to find some lunch," he said. "It's nearly three and I haven't eaten anything since breakfast."

"Good idea. I don't want to wear you out."

Derek grabbed her by the waist and tossed her into the deep end of the pool. He wasn't sure what course this relationship would take over the next few days. But he did know exactly where he wanted this all to end—with Tess in his bed, in his life, for a long time to come.

AFTER A QUICK SHOWER, they drove over to the resort restaurant for an early dinner. The open-air dining room was almost empty and the waiter gave them a secluded table that overlooked the beach. No matter where she was on the island, Tess found herself captivated by the view—white sand, turquoise water and a sky so blue, it hurt to look at it.

She sipped at a virgin piña colada as the waiter set their meal in front of them. Derek sat next to her, dressed in a thin cotton shirt and board shorts. The shirt was unbuttoned halfway down his chest and Tess had to fight the urge to smooth her hand over his deeply tanned skin. She loved to touch him whenever she felt the urge. But for the first time since Chloe had left, they weren't alone.

Her stomach growled as the scent of the seafood pasta she'd ordered drifted up from the plate. She hadn't eaten anything but an apple since breakfast that morning, six hours before.

"I'm sorry about that thing with Alicia," Derek said, smoothing his hand along her thigh as he kissed her bare shoulder.

"If she comes to the island, she better watch out. I'm good with my fists. She won't be able to get you away from me."

"I'd pay to see that," he teased. "Especially if it involved mud and a lot of hair-pulling and screaming."

Tess set her drink down and picked up her fork. "I'm starved. Sex works up such an appetite." She took a bite of her pasta and moaned. "Oh, this is so good. We have to come back here again. There were four or five things on the menu I wanted to try."

"You can order anything you want and have it delivered to the house," he said.

"Really?"

"Anytime you want, day or night. Just dial nine." He picked up his burger and took a bite. "So, tell me more about this fight you're going to have with Alicia. Give me details. I want to picture it in my mind."

"Pervert!" Tess cried.

"I bet you're pretty scrappy. You look like you could hold your own in a fight."

Tess tipped up her chin and pointed. "See this scar. Sixth grade, playground. I punched Billy Carlisle. Twice. In the nose. Blood everywhere. Then he punched me back. Two stitches and I got sent home by the principal." She pointed to her knee. "I got this in a fight with

Sally Armstrong. She called me a name and I threw my Backstreet Boys lunchbox at her. She pushed me down on the sidewalk and I cut my knee on a piece of glass."

"Why did you fight so much?"

"I was always the odd girl," she said. "Moving into a new school every six months or so. We didn't have money for nice clothes. There were weeks that we lived out of the back of our pickup truck while my dad was looking for work. I didn't have a mom. A lot of kids saw that as weakness and they thought they could take advantage of me. I proved they couldn't."

"That's not a very happy story," he said. "I wish you hadn't had to go through that."

"It taught me a lot. I'm not scared of a challenge," she explained. "I almost expect it. I can never really trust that things will just turn out fine. I managed to get over Jeffrey in less than a day. I consider that a major accomplishment."

"I hope I had a little bit to do with that."

Tess nodded. "Just a little bit," she murmured.

He grabbed her hand and kissed the back of her wrist. A thrill raced through her. When he'd invited her to the island, Tess had thought it would be so simple. A place to escape and time to think about her future. But all that had changed. Tess knew that what was happening between her and Derek was far from simple.

Even though she didn't want to love him, how could she keep from feeling something deeper when he seemed to see into the deepest corners of her soul? She kept telling herself they'd go back to their lives soon enough, but in her dreams, their vacation would be endless.

"Tonight is New Year's Eve," Derek said. "What would you like to do?"

"I don't know," Tess said. "What are our options?"

"We could stay here. There are fireworks planned and we'll be able to watch them from the beach. Or we could go across to Frenchman's Cay. My family owns the resort there and I'm sure there's a big party planned. Dancing, good food, a big celebration at midnight. Or I could call the plane. We could go anywhere you like."

"So many choices," she murmured. Tess never felt as if she'd had many choices in her life. She had been ready to marry a man she didn't love simply to provide financial security for her family. How easy life must have been for Derek.

Tess's gaze dropped down to her plate. Though they shared a few life experiences, they weren't alike at all. She'd had to fight for every good thing that happened to her and he'd had it all handed to him. That thought seemed only to emphasize the real distance between them.

"What are you thinking?" he asked.

"Fireworks," she said. "Just you and me. On the beach."

"I'll make it something special," he said. "We'll have our own little celebration."

"We'll have to make resolutions. We can't start the New Year without a few resolutions."

"I don't even bother with those." He grabbed one of

the sweet potato chips next to his burger and munched on it. "But I suppose I could come up with something."

"I make one every year."

"And what was last year's?" Derek asked.

"I promised myself I'd ride every day. I was so busy managing the farm that I kind of forgot how much fun it was to ride. I bought a mare a few years back—Genny—and she'd been stuck walking in circles on the horse exerciser. I felt bad."

"Did you keep the resolution?"

Tess nodded. "Yes, I did. I think I only missed three or four days. And then she foaled and I missed a couple weeks. This weekend is the longest I've been away from the farm. We go out in rain and snow, her colt trailing after us."

"Maybe, someday, you can teach me how to ride."

Someday, Tess thought to herself. That word was much more complicated than it appeared on the surface. It signaled the possibility of a future. Did she really want to allow herself that kind of fantasy? "Maybe," she replied. "What about you? What kind of resolutions do you make?"

"They all have to do with work. I'll finish my travel reports on time, I'll be more careful packing for trips, I'll learn Japanese. All very boring and impossible to keep."

"And what will you promise for this year?"

Derek considered her question, his brow furrowing as he thought. "I don't know. I'll come up with something good. Maybe this year, it'll work out. What about you?"

"I'm giving up men," Tess said.

Derek laughed, then picked up his beer and took a long drink. "Really? So after midnight, I'm history?"

"No, not you. I'm staying away from relationships. They're too complicated. I like what we have. It's simple and straightforward."

"So when does what we have turn into a relationship?"

"When we start talking about the future," she said.

He stared at her, his gaze searching hers. Tess knew her answer had been insensitive. It wasn't difficult to imagine that he might want more. It was easy for him. He could fly in and out of her life on a whim. She was the one who had to live in the real world, working at a job she wasn't sure she still had.

Tess hadn't bothered to consider what was going to happen to her position at the farm once she got back. Would Jeffrey feel compelled to fire her? Or would he expect her to continue on with their secret affair? There weren't many other choices. She wasn't brave enough to quit, at least not without another job lined up. Maybe that would be her New Year's resolution—to look for a new job.

"I don't want to think about the future," Tess said, shaking her head. "I just want to enjoy each minute we spend here."

"I'm cool with that," Derek replied.

"Good." Tess pointed to his plate. "Can I try one of those chips? They look really good."

They finished their meal and then Derek took her on a tour of the resort. She was surprised at how small and simple it was, just a quaint collection of buildings built on low stilts with palm frond roofs. He steered her toward a small cluster of huts near the guest services center, a collection of shops filled with expensive items that rich people might need on their vacation.

Tess browsed through racks of pretty summer dresses and swimsuits while Derek chatted with the store manager, but when she checked the tags, she realized everything in the store was well out of her price range.

"Have you found anything you like?" Derek asked.

"Plenty," she said. "But I don't need anything. I have the dresses you got from Chloe."

"But those aren't very fancy." He pulled a gauzy white dress from the rack and held it out, the jeweled neckline sparkling beneath the light. "How about this one?"

"No," she said.

"No, you don't like it?"

"No, it's ridiculously expensive. I'm very practical, Derek. I'd have no place to wear it after tonight."

"Stop being practical. And this dress isn't for you. It's for me."

"You're going to wear it?"

"No, I'm going to admire you in it."

"I thought you preferred me naked," Tess teased,

trying desperately to change the subject. "Come on, let's go."

"Really," he insisted. "I want get you something for tonight. Your choice."

"I don't want you to buy me anything," Tess said, a stubborn edge in her voice. "That wasn't part of our deal."

"We didn't really make a deal," Derek said. He pulled another dress from the rack, a short floral mini with a halter neckline. The layers of sheer fabric on the skirt looked like petals, moving in the breeze. "I like this one. You look pretty in blue."

She looked at the tag. "It's four hundred dollars." Tess laughed. "I don't think so."

"Yeah, but I get a family discount."

"How much?" she asked.

"Free," he said.

"No."

"Really. Ask the clerk. Half the stuff I gave you from Chloe's closet was stuff she took out of this shop. So what's the difference? You can wear it once and leave it in her closet, if you'd like. She'd never know."

The dress was pretty, Tess mused, fingering the fabric. And this was a special celebration. She wanted to please him, to look nice for their party. And if she left it on the island for Chloe, she wouldn't feel nearly as guilty. She'd be borrowing it. "All right, then. I'll take it."

"Shoes, too," he said.

"Chloe can't wear shoes that aren't her size. And I

haven't worn shoes since we got here. The ones I have will be fine. If you really want to buy me something, buy me underwear."

"No underwear," he said, shaking his head. "But a necklace would be nice. And earrings."

Reluctantly, Tess allowed Derek to choose her jewelry. At first, it made her uneasy, taking gifts from him. But he was right. This entire fantasy had been a gift and it hadn't come cheap. She could swallow her pride in order to make Derek happy.

In the end, she walked away with the dress, a pretty necklace with a matching pair of earrings, and a bangle bracelet. As they walked back to the Range Rover, Tess wondered if this was what a future with Derek would be like.

He was sweet and generous and never had to think before spending money. It wasn't his fault she didn't know how to accept a gift. There had been so few of them in her lifetime. Most everything that had been given to her came with strings attached.

"Thank you," Tess said, slipping her arm through his. "I love the dress."

He kissed the top of her head. "You're welcome. And you'll look beautiful in it."

DEREK STOOD AT THE MIRROR in his bathroom and ran his fingers through his damp hair. After they'd returned from their meal, Tess had insisted that she have time to get ready for their New Year's celebration. Unfortunately, that had included a long nap, alone, in her own bed.

Though he'd tried to convince her they'd be able to nap together, even he knew what would happen once they crawled into bed. He'd never be able to keep his hands to himself. So he'd taken a long run, then dozed at the pool as the sun began to set.

It was New Year's Eve and for the first time in five years, he had a date with a beautiful woman. He'd called the resort staff and they'd set everything up on the beach—flowers, food, music. He'd wanted the setting to be perfect, hoping that Tess might realize what he had already—that this thing between them might be more than just a passing fantasy.

After Alicia, Derek had been very careful not to get involved, not to commit himself to something he wasn't ready to sustain. But Tess had changed all that. He didn't want to return her to her life without some promise of seeing her again.

He grabbed his watch and strapped it on his wrist, slipped some extra condoms in his pocket, then took one last look at his reflection. The gauzy cotton shirt and the drawstring pants weren't typically what he'd wear on New Year's Eve, but the less he had on, the better. No underwear was the dress code for the evening.

When he got to Tess's room, it was empty. He walked inside and called her name, then heard her reply from behind the bathroom door.

"I—I'll be out…in…in a minute," she said.

Her voice was muffled and it sounded as if she was

upset. He listened at the door and heard her sniffle. "Tess, let me in." He tried the door, but it was locked. "Tess? Come on. Unlock the door."

"I'm almost done," she called impatiently.

"Please, open the door." Derek waited, listening for a response. When the lock clicked, he opened the door to find her sitting on the edge of the tub, a wad of tissue in her hand. Her eyes were red and her nose was runny.

He sat down beside her. "What's wrong?"

"Look at me!" she said, angrily brushing tears from her cheeks. She stood up and crossed to the mirror, then spun around.

"I am looking at you," Derek said, confused. Was she unhappy with the dress? Was there something wrong with her hair? Maybe she needed some underwear after all? "You're beautiful."

"I know!" she shouted. "I'm beautiful. Even *I* think I'm beautiful and I never think that. My hair, I don't know what's going on with that. It never looks this good. And this dress makes me look glamorous. I have a tan and freckles on my nose. I don't even need to put on makeup." The tears started again and she picked up her skirt in her fists. "And I'm not wearing any underwear and I don't care."

"I don't see what the problem is," Derek said.

"How am I supposed to go back to my old life? How am I supposed to be happy with what I have?" She picked up a small tag and waved it under his nose. "Four hundred dollars. That's what this dress cost."

Derek grabbed the tag from her. "I thought we settled this."

"You don't even have to look at the price tag. I've never in my life bought clothes that weren't on a sale rack. And then I wear them until they're completely worn out. I've always had to think about how much I could safely spend and you—well, you just don't even have think."

"I'm sorry," Derek said. "You don't have to wear the dress. I'll take it back. I just liked the color and I knew it would look nice on you."

"No, I love the dress." She turned and looked at her reflection in the mirror, smoothing her hands over her hips. "I love it."

This was the most confusing conversation he'd ever had with a woman. What did she want? No matter what he suggested, it brought a fresh round of tears. "Then what's the problem?"

"The problem is, I like myself better when I look like this. And when I feel like this. When I'm laughing and having fun. And kissing you and touching you. I'm happier than I've ever been. And it scares me that it's all going to end and I'm never going to be this happy again."

"I don't know what to say."

A ragged sigh slipped from her throat. "It's like losing something I never thought I wanted."

Derek gathered her into his arms. "I just want you to be happy, Tess. What can I do to make you smile again?"

"You could kiss me," she said. "That helps."

He wiped the tears from her cheeks with his thumbs and then touched his lips to hers. God, there was something about kissing her that just felt so good. It wasn't about need or desire or sex. It was just the simplest form of communication between the two of them.

Derek kissed one eye and then the other before nuzzling her nose. "Better?"

"Yes," she said, drawing in a ragged breath. "I'm sorry." She laughed. "I'd never survive living like this. Who am I kidding? I go to bed at nine every night and get up at dawn. I'm a fish out of water here."

"And how do you think I'd feel on a horse farm? I don't know one end of a horse from another."

Tess laughed. "I'm sure you'd figure it out pretty fast."

He loved that he was able to move her from tears to laughter in the matter of a minute. "But you understand what I'm saying, right? Just because we come from different places doesn't mean we can't be together." He grabbed her hand and pulled her out of the bathroom. "Come on, our party is waiting on the beach."

They walked through the room and outside into the darkness. It was a perfect night—the sky was clear and filled with stars, and a soft breeze was blowing in from the ocean. Derek wrapped his arm around her shoulders and tucked her against his body as they strolled. "We've been here for twenty-four hours. I don't think I've ever packed so much into a single day."

"I could stay here forever," she said.

Derek kissed the top of her head. "We can do that."

"In some alternate universe maybe. But not in the one I live in. I'm going to have to go home. Sunday at the latest."

"So we have another day and night after this. And after that?"

Tess shook her head. "Let's not try to figure out anything beyond this island," she said.

They came over the rise and Tess stopped short at the view. As instructed, the resort staff had devised the most romantic setting they could possibly provide and it had exactly the right effect on her.

"Oh, my God," she said, turning to look at him. "What have you done?"

Derek grinned. "I made a few phone calls. I guess the staff took a personal interest in this."

The beach was scattered with lanterns, all of them flickering in the breeze. A tent made of sheer netting was furnished with a bed, which was draped in white linens and soft pillows. Music drifted through the air from an unknown source and a small platform for dancing with a dinner table laden with things to eat and drink had even been provided.

Tess hurried ahead of him, taking in the elaborate setting. Pushing aside the netting, she stepped inside the tent. He followed her, standing beside her as she picked at a tray of chocolates and fresh berries on the bedside table. "Look at this," she said. "Chocolate truffles. And fresh raspberries." She fed him a truffle, then took one for herself. "You're right," she said. "This is nothing like a horse farm."

He spanned her waist with his hands and guided her out of the tent. "I think we should dance," he said.

"I don't really dance," Tess said. "I've never been to a dance in my life."

"Never?"

"I didn't go in high school. No one ever asked me. I can sway, but that's about it."

Derek wrapped his arm around her waist and pulled their hips together. "Everyone can dance. If you can ride a horse, you can dance."

"Yes. But I grew up around horses."

He slowly began to move with the music. They'd moved in the same easy rhythm in bed that morning. Tess began to follow along with him. "See, it's easy."

"Are you sure this isn't about something else?" she asked. "It feels an awful lot like…"

"Like what?"

"Foreplay," she said.

"Well, it is. It's a universal mode of foreplay. Accompanied by music. When we move like this, our bodies together, touching, my hands just slowly caressing you. It's supposed to remind you of something. All we have to do is get horizontal and there you are. Sex."

Tess laughed. "And we just happen to have a bed right over there. How handy is that?"

"Just go with the beat." He held her hand. "And now we'll twirl."

She spun out with a little scream and he turned her beneath his arm and pulled her back into his embrace. "Now comes the dip," he warned. He dropped her back, then pulled her up again. Her face was so close to his that he snuck a quick kiss. But just one kiss wasn't enough.

As they continued to dance, Derek kissed her again, her lips parting beneath his on a sigh. The music faded as his pulse began to quicken. They gradually stopped moving until they were both caught up in his greedy exploration of her mouth.

He smoothed his palm along her hips, then bunched the skirt of her dress in his hands until he could feel the warm flesh beneath.

"You bought me a dress, but you didn't buy me underwear," she explained. "It is rather…liberating."

"Maybe later we can liberate you from that dress."

Tess laughed, her arms wrapped around his neck, her body pressed against his. "I'm already getting tired of wearing it."

Derek brushed his lips across hers. How would he ever find another woman like Tess? Everything they shared was so much fun. Though there had been serious moments, they'd passed quickly and without silly hysterics.

She'd called herself practical and at first, he hadn't attached anything positive to the quality. It made her sincere and down-to-earth. She had no artifice or ego. There might be a lot about Tess Robertson that Derek didn't know yet, but he knew she was the real deal. And he was beginning to believe that it was the one thing he loved most about her.

6

A BREEZE SNAPPED AT the netting of the tent and waves crashed against the shore, drawing Derek out of a deep and dreamless sleep. He rolled over onto his stomach, pressing his face into the down pillow and reaching out for Tess. But her side of the bed was empty.

He sat up and raked his hands through his hair, remembering their celebration the night before. They'd danced and laughed and entertained each other with silly stories of their youth. At midnight, beneath the fireworks, they'd stripped off their clothes and run into the surf, playing like carefree teenagers in the warm water. After exhausting themselves, they had crawled into bed and made slow, sweet love until the sun began to lighten the eastern sky.

Derek squinted out at the horizon, then noticed Tess wading at the water's edge fifty yards down the beach. She was naked, her slender limbs gleaming in the sunlight. She held a stick and was staring at something beneath the surface, looking like some sea nymph, all luscious curves and tousled hair.

Derek tossed aside the bed linens and stood up, stretching his arm above his head as he walked out onto the sand. They had another twenty-four hours together. Today, he'd make arrangements for their flight back and try to figure out a way to keep her in his life just a little bit longer.

As he strolled toward her, he noticed a drawing in wet sand and stopped to look at it. She'd drawn a huge heart and placed their initials inside it. But the tide had already begun to wash it away. It was a perfect metaphor—the passion between them was just temporary, like a drawing in the sand.

"What are you doing out here?"

She turned to face him, then smiled. "Nothing. Just thinking."

He slipped his arms around her waist and gave her a gentle kiss. "Happy New Year."

Tess laughed. "Very happy New Year."

"What are you thinking about?"

"It's our last day here," she said. "It went so fast."

"We've only been here for a day and a half," he said. "That's why it went fast. But we can stay longer. Just say the word."

She shook her head. "No. I have to get back. I don't want to, but I have to."

"What if I refuse to take you back? We could build a little hut on the beach and live here forever. We'd never have to wear clothes again."

"Now, that's a nice fantasy," she said. "I really could live just like this."

"What do we really need? Our little hut, a few hammocks. We could live pretty cheaply. Or, if you'd rather, we could take the boat and sail around the world. I've always dreamed about doing that." He kissed her shoulder. "What do you dream about?"

"I don't think it's always good to dwell on things you can't have."

"But if you could have anything in the world, what would you want? Money is no object."

"Oh, this is one of *those* fantasies," she said. "The one where I win the lottery and have a hundred million dollars at my disposal."

"Yes," he said. "What would you do?"

"I'd buy a farm. And I'd run it the way I wanted to. I'd breed the best thoroughbreds in Kentucky. Or maybe Virginia. I'd like to live in Virginia."

"Why not do it? You could start small."

"Horse breeding is just a license to burn money," she said. "You have to have so much that if you lose a lot of it, it doesn't make a difference. But I guess I could have a little farm of my own. I could do that."

"How is it going to be when you get back?"

Tess shrugged. "I don't know. Probably not good. I can't imagine Jeffrey will want me to continue on at the farm. Unless, of course, he expects nothing to change."

Derek felt tension snake through his body. Would she really consider continuing her affair with her boss just to keep her job? "Things have changed," he said. "What do you want?"

Drawing a deep breath, she pasted a smile on her face. "I want to not think about this today and deal with it tomorrow. Today, I just want to have fun. Like we did last night."

"All right. So, why don't we sail over to Abaco for lunch. Maybe stop by the casino before heading back. Or do a little snorkeling. There are some shops there, too, if you'd like to buy something to remember our trip."

"Oh, I don't need a T-shirt to remember this place," she said, staring out at the turquoise water. "It's burned into my memory."

"What about me? Will you forget me?"

"That would be impossible, too." She yawned, then pressed her face into his chest. "I need coffee and a long hot shower."

He took her hand and led her back to the tent. As they passed her heart drawn in the sand, Derek noticed it was almost washed away. He made a mental note to come back to this very spot after she'd left and redraw it, hoping the sentiment might be real enough to last.

They didn't bother to stop for their clothes, walking up the path without even thinking of retrieving them. When they reached her room, Derek went into the large bathroom and turned on the shower, then pulled her beneath the warm spray.

As his hands smoothed over her body, he couldn't help but feel a surge of desire. Would there ever come a time when he didn't want her? When they'd completely exhausted their need for each other? The prospect of waking up alone, without her beside him, was almost unimaginable. Casual sex with any other woman would never satisfy him again.

Derek closed his eyes as the water rushed over him. He felt her palm smoothing over his chest and smiled. Grabbing her waist, Derek pulled her into a deep and demanding kiss.

Tess ran her hands over his back. "You've turned me into a lazy bum," she said. "I sleep too much, drink too much, eat too much and lie around all day long. I haven't done a single productive thing since you put me on that plane."

"You want to do something productive?" he asked.

"Yes. It might be nice for a change."

"Wash my back." He handed her the soap and turned around.

He waited while she lathered her hands, but she didn't stop with his back. Instead, she reached around and wrapped her fingers around his semi-hard cock. Derek groaned. "Yes, I guess that might be considered productive, too." He turned and nuzzled her neck. "You are going to wear me out."

"You'll have plenty of time to recover after I've gone," she said, her caress arousing him completely with just a few strokes.

He leaned back against the marble wall, then reached down to touch the spot between her legs. If she wanted to tease him like this, then turnabout was fair play. The desire that had surrounded them since they'd first met hadn't diminished. In truth, it had only increased, becoming more intense as their fantasy came closer to ending.

He knew exactly how she liked it. He could read her response and sense when she was close. But it was more difficult to concentrate when she was stroking him. Delicious sensations coursed through his body.

Tess's pace quickened and Derek didn't realize how close he was. Suddenly, his need peaked and his body dissolved into a powerful orgasm, so intense it surprised him. Maybe it was the water or her slick hand, or just the feel of her wet body moving against his, but his release went on and on, each spasm more forceful than the last.

He was so lost in his own pleasure that he didn't realize she'd reached her own release. Tess moaned softly, then dissolved into shudders, her body falling against his.

They continued to touch each other, slowly drifting back to reality. And when she was completely sated, he pulled her into his embrace as they both stood beneath the rushing water. What was he going to do without her?

They dried each other off with thick cotton towels. Derek wrapped one around his waist and walked back to his room to get dressed, leaving her to finish getting ready. As he walked across the courtyard, she leaned over the railing and gave him a piercing wolf whistle. "Hey, baby, looking good."

Chuckling to himself, he pulled the towel off and

tossed it over his shoulder, giving her a view worth the whistle. He turned and held out his hands. "I know you love me," he shouted.

Though the words were chosen quickly, before he realized they could be misconstrued, Derek didn't care. He was falling in love with Tess and he found nothing wrong with the possibility that by the end of their time together, he'd be hopelessly entangled.

"It's about time," he murmured, climbing the stairs to his room. He'd been waiting around for something to change in his life and now it had. In the course of just a few minutes, spent in an elevator, he'd found something worth keeping. And he damn well wasn't going to let her get away.

THE RIDE ACROSS THE WATER was both exhilarating and terrifying all at once. Tess had never been in a sailboat, much less a boat on open water. But with the spray hitting her face and the wind blowing through her hair, she felt completely at home.

"It's like riding," she called to Derek.

He stood behind the wheel in the cockpit, steering the boat towards a long, low island on the horizon. He looked so handsome, dressed in khaki shorts, a bright green polo shirt and deck shoes. His eyes were hidden by his sunglasses, but she knew he'd been watching her.

She'd stretched out in the cockpit, on one of the cushioned seats, her cotton dress pulled up over her thighs, her body naked beneath. The sun felt glorious on her skin and she'd already managed a decent tan. It was hard to believe she'd be back in cold, damp Kentucky by the end of the day tomorrow. But she'd decided not to regret a single minute spent with Derek, even if it made her life back home seem less than ideal.

She was lucky to have lived out a fantasy. How often could you run away from your problems? Her time with Derek actually made her feel stronger, better equipped to handle what was waiting for her back home.

"Do you want to steer?" he asked.

Tess nodded, then jumped up and stood between him and the huge wheel. He pointed to the compass, explaining their heading, then showed her how to keep the sail filled with air. The wind was at their back and the water was choppy. But the sleek sailboat cut smoothly through the waves at an impressive speed.

"I'm going to trim the jib," he said. "Just stay on this heading."

Tess screamed as he stepped away from her, but she remembered his instructions and managed to keep the boat at the proper heading. When he returned, he sat down and crossed his legs in front of him, stretching his arms on the back of the seat.

"You're doing fine," he said.

"I'm sailing a boat," Tess cried.

"You are."

"This is fun. So what happens if the wind changes?"

"You just adjust the sail, pull it in or let it out to catch the most air." He stared out at the water, then pointed to the port side. "Look. Dolphins."

She scanned the area, but as she turned, she pulled the wheel along with her. When the boat veered, Tess yanked the wheel in the other direction. Derek jumped up and stepped behind her, righting their course as the boom snapped back into place.

"Sorry," she said, gripping the wheel in white-knuckled hands.

He wrapped his arms around her waist, drawing her body back against his and resting his chin on her shoulder. "Watch the little red stripes on the edge of the main sail," he explained. "Those should be blowing straight back. Turn a bit more to port."

"Which is port?" she asked.

"Left," he said. "Port and left have the same number of letters. That's how you remember."

By the time they reached the harbor on Abaco, Tess had learned more about sailing than she ever thought there was to know. She worked the winches to trim the sails and learned how to tack. And she'd even radioed the harbormaster at the resort, informing him of their arrival.

A young man in a white uniform was waiting as they motored into the inlet, the sails down. Tess tossed him the bow line and he tied it up, then moved to catch the line that Derek held at the back of the boat. When the boat was secure, she grabbed her sandals and hopped off onto the dock.

"The Jeep is waiting in the car park, Mr. Nolan," the dockhand said. "Keys are in it."

"Thanks," Derek said, grabbing Tess's hand.

"Is there anything you don't own around here?"

He looked around. "That sailboat over there," he said seriously, causing her to laugh.

They found the Jeep, and before long they were speeding along the narrow island roads, Tess watching Derek as he drove. Upon first meeting him, she had thought he was handsome. More than just ordinarily handsome. But as she'd grown to know him, she found herself fixated on the tiny details of his appearance. The way the corners of his mouth curled up to make two dimples when he smiled. Or the way his hair always managed to look like he'd just stepped out of a windstorm. Or the way his long fingers smoothed the back of his neck when he was thinking about something.

The sound of his laugh, the color of his eyes, the way he moved with an easy grace that made him seem so powerful—all of these things had become qualities she found endearing. And though Tess had tried to focus on the broader picture, again and again, she found herself committing silly details to her memory and then turning them over and over in her mind.

He glanced at her and noticed her staring, then reached out and slipped his arm around her shoulders. "You'll like this place," he said. "It's where all the locals go when they want something good to eat. They serve real island food."

Tess nodded, then turned to look at the landscape passing by. This could be her life, she mused. Exploring the world with Derek, seeing new places and meeting new people, every day a new adventure. There was so much she hadn't experienced and until this moment, she'd never realized it.

Life on the farm was all about day-to-day survival, paying the bills and keeping her job and placating the owners when things fell apart. When business was going well, she and her father never got the credit. That always went to someone else.

How nice it would be to not have to worry about her future—to just look forward to the next day and the day after that, all sunshine and lollipops as her father liked to say. A long string of beautiful days spinning out in front of her with nothing but adventure on the agenda.

"I love this," Tess shouted. She threw up her hands and screamed. "I love this!"

She looked over at Derek and he laughed, ruffling her windblown hair. A few moments later, he pulled off the road and onto a narrow dirt lane. A ramshackle outdoor pavilion appeared behind a grove of trees. He parked the Jeep, then turned off the ignition. But before he could speak, Tess threw herself into his arms and kissed him.

"Thank you," she said. "For bringing me here. For showing me all this."

He glanced around at the flat landscape, the over-grown brush and the tall grass. "This?"

"All of it," she said. "I'm never going to forget the last few days. They've been the most perfect ones of my life." She sat back in her seat. "Let's go, I'm hungry!"

It wasn't really a restaurant in the traditional sense, Tess thought as they approached. Just a tin roof held up by four wooden pillars with a hodgepodge of tables and chairs scattered beneath.

The people who ran the place welcomed them both with smiles and happy greetings and seated them at a table with a red vinyl tablecloth. All the food was cooked outside on a long grill. Pots simmered at one end and a delicious array of meats and vegetables were grilled on the other.

The owner, a tall black man with sparkling eyes, brought them a bottle of the house wine, then pulled out a pad to take their order. "Give us your best, Joe," Derek said. "My girl is hungry."

"I'll bring you somethin' special," he said with a chuckle. "You gonna like it a lot."

They sipped their wine from old jelly jars as course after course arrived—conch chowder followed by coconut shrimp followed by a dish of plantains and spicy chicken, surrounded by fresh vegetables. And for dessert they had a creamy mango tart.

They talked and laughed, enjoying the food almost as much as they were enjoying each other's company. Derek told her stories about the exotic places he'd visited and the interesting foods he'd eaten. She told him about the year one of their horses ran in the Kentucky Derby.

He took such delight in listening to her tell a story. Even when she was babbling on about something silly, Derek was staring into her eyes and asking her question after question.

It was nearly dark when Derek paid the bill. They

walked back to the Jeep, his arm draped around her shoulders, her body pulled close to his. Thunder rumbled and Tess saw lightning flash in the distance. "It can't rain," she said.

"It occasionally does in paradise," Derek answered. "Look at those clouds. We won't be going back to the island until the storm passes."

"Why not?"

"If I take you out in rough weather, you may never want to sail again. We'll leave that for another time. Besides, there's so much more to do here. We can shop or go to the casino or just hole up in a room and mess around."

"Just like that," she said. "Is life ever difficult for you?"

He thought about her question for a long moment. "I guess I take a lot of things for granted. You're right. I should be more aware of what I have." He pulled her closer and kissed the top of her head. "When I forget, you need to remind me."

"After I go home, I'll just text you every few days. Just so you keep it real."

He opened the door of the Jeep and helped her inside, then leaned over and kissed her through the open window. "All right. It's a deal."

THE CASINO AT THE RESORT was teeming with activity. Derek had thought it would be fun for Tess, but he could tell she was a bit overwhelmed by the noise. As they walked past the slots, her gaze darted from one spot to another, silently observing what was going on.

"We won't stay long," he said.

She nodded. "No, it's all right. This looks like fun."

"Have you ever been to a casino?" he asked.

Tess shook her head. "I've been to the track. Sometimes for races that our horses have run in. More often, to drag my father home after one of his gambling binges. But I'm not much of a gambler. I always place a two-dollar bet on our horses when they run. But that's not gambling—it's superstition."

As they strolled through, Derek realized that the place suffered in comparison to the peace and quiet of the island. Until he'd met Tess, he'd always felt comfortable in a noisy atmosphere. It kept his thoughts occupied, kept him from feeling lonely. But now Derek much preferred a quiet spot with Tess, a place where he could talk to her and hold her hand. A place he could kiss her and touch her without people watching.

"We'll play roulette," he said. They stopped at the cashier's window and he signed for two one-thousand-dollar chips, then handed her one.

Tess looked at him, then pushed the chip back at him. "No," she said. "I'm not going to be responsible for losing a thousand dollars. If you want to throw away your money like that, I have a few horse farms you can invest in."

"Take it," he said. "If you win, you can pay me back. We're each going to place one bet, just like you do at the track, and then we're going to get the hell out of here."

"Remember when I promised to tell you to keep it real. This is one of those times. A thousand dollars is a lot of money. More than I make in a week of work."

"But you're forgetting that my family owns this casino. So basically, I'm taking the money they pay me to work for the family business and I'm giving it back to the family business." She frowned as she sorted through his explanation. "It's all the same money," Derek continued. "If I lose, the family business makes more. If I win, they make less. But I hardly ever win."

Tess shook her head adamantly. "No. I can't."

"All right," Derek said. "I feel lucky. I've been feeling lucky since the moment you stepped on that elevator."

When they got to the roulette table, he explained the game to her, showing her how he could bet on individual numbers or bet on all the reds or all the blacks, or even or odd numbers. "Whenever I'm here, I always place a bet on black thirteen," Derek said.

He placed one of the chips on the square and stood back, waiting as the croupier started the wheel and spun the marble along the edge. He glanced over at Tess and found her holding her breath, a worried expression on her beautiful face.

The ball landed in red thirty-two and Tess moaned. "That's it? That's all you get out of it? It happens so fast. At least with the horses, you get to watch a two-minute race."

Derek shrugged. "Yeah. But it's a rush when you win."

"Have you ever won?"

He nodded. "Once. At our casino in Vegas. A one-thousand dollar bet on one number pays thirty-five thousand."

"Holy shit," Tess said. She clapped her hand to her mouth, then glanced around. "Sorry. Thirty-five thousand dollars?"

He pointed to the table. "Are you sure you don't want to give it try? If you win, just pay me back my thousand and you keep the winnings. Remember, you're supporting the Nolan family by betting."

Tess relented and took the chip from him. "All right. Should I put it on your number?"

"You could. But maybe you should choose a number that means something to you."

She searched the table looking for a good number, then settled on one. "Red twenty-seven," she said. "Because it's my age and the color of the racing silks at the farm."

"Go ahead," he said. "Put the bet down."

Tess placed the chip on the table, then turned and buried her face in Derek's chest. "I can't watch."

"That's the fun," he said. "Waiting for the ball to drop."

"If I had an extra thousand dollars, I'd fix my truck. Or buy a new saddle. Or boots. I need new boots."

"But just think what you could do with thirty-five thousand," he said, rubbing her back.

There were times when all he wanted to do was protect her, to be that person in her life she could always depend upon. As he glanced around at the others standing at the roulette table, Derek wondered what they were thinking about him and Tess. Did they assume they were married or maybe a couple? Even he wouldn't have believed they'd met only a day ago.

"I'm just going to consider this another new experience," Tess said. "I won't think of it as money. It's just a pretty little chip."

Derek watched the croupier as he started the wheel, then sent the marble spinning. He bent down and kissed the top of Tess's head, chuckling softly. But when everyone began to scream, Derek looked up. "Holy shit," he muttered.

Tess turned. "Did someone win?"

He laughed and pointed at the table. "Yeah, someone won. You did. It's red twenty-seven."

Tess hurried to the edge of the table and stared at the marble resting in the slot on the wheel. The croupier pushed aside all the other chips and began to stack chips in a little plastic tray. "Congratulations," he said.

"I won?"

He nodded. When he was finished stacking her chips, he stepped back.

"Go ahead," Derek said. "Take your winnings."

Tess frowned and looked up at him. "Did you make that wheel stop where it did? Just so I could win?"

"Are you crazy? No, I didn't fix the game. You won, fair and square. Although, I don't know how it happened." He reached out and grabbed the tray and handed it to her. "I'm taking my stake back.

"Kiss this chip," he said.

Tess did as she was told and he set the chip on his favorite number and waited for the next spin. But once again, the marble found a different slot and Derek lost. "Oh, well," he said to the crowd surrounding the table. "Lucky in love, unlucky at roulette."

They walked back to the cashier's window with her winnings and Tess watched, wide-eyed, as they counted out her winnings and placed it in front of her. Then the cashier put the money in an envelope and handed it to Tess. "Would you like me to call security for an escort?" she asked.

Tess glanced nervously up at Derek. "No," he said, shaking his head. "I'll keep an eye on her."

"Why did they ask that?" she murmured as they walked out. "Is someone going to rob me?"

"No. But some of our clients might have a little too much to drink and we just want to make sure they don't misplace any of their winnings. An escort is offered to all our winners."

She handed him the envelope. "I don't like carrying so much money. It makes me nervous. You keep it."

"But it's yours."

She shook her head. "No. Believe me, I wish it was, but it's not mine. I didn't work for it. It's not right. And it doesn't even seem real."

Derek didn't want to argue with her. "Okay. Whatever you want. But it was your luck that won the money."

"It was your money in the first place."

Money seemed to be a sore point with her, Derek mused. He'd never met a woman who was totally uninterested in his wealth. Tess seemed almost afraid of it, as if it were a negative in their relationship. Though he'd gotten a good sense of the struggles she'd gone through in her life, he didn't completely understand why she wouldn't welcome a bit of relief from her worries. Thirty-four thousand dollars would have gone a long way to buying the little farm she'd dreamed about.

"I'm glad we're going back," Tess said.

"Why is that?"

"Because I like the quiet of the island." She wrapped her arms around him. "It's just us. And there's nothing else but us to think about."

When they reached the dock, Derek jumped into the cockpit, then held out his hand to help Tess onto the boat. He wrapped his arms around her and indulged in a long, deep kiss. "I want you to promise me something," he said when he finally drew back.

"What?"

"No matter what happens between us, I want you to promise that if you ever need help, you'll call me."

"Derek, I've—"

"No. No argument. I know you've taken care of yourself and done fine. But there may come a day when that's not possible. And I want you to know you can count on me to help you, Tess. I will always want you to be happy and I'll do anything to make sure you are."

She stared up at him, her face luminous from the lights on the dock. "All right," she finally said, nodding.

"Promise."

"I promise."

Derek smiled. "Good." He looked up at the stars overhead. "I think we can sail back. It doesn't look like the weather is going to bother us. Do you want to go?"

She nodded. "Take me back to our island," Tess said.

Derek worked quickly getting the boat ready to go. Though visiting civilization might have been a pleasant diversion, Tess was right. They seemed to be much happier when it was just the two of them.

Would that be the case if they tried to continue their relationship after she left? Would the real world always seem like a comedown from paradise? Derek wanted to believe they had a future together. He needed to know he'd continue to be a part of her life.

He was almost afraid to broach the subject with her. Tess had seemed so adamant about the fantasy ending when she left. And he understood her reluctance to consider a future with him. They lived in two completely different worlds. But they had found common ground on the island. Why couldn't that happen back in Kentucky? Or in San Diego? Or anywhere they decided to be together?

"It's a beautiful night," he said as they motored out of the inlet. "Come here and help me steer."

Tess joined him at the wheel, slipping into his embrace as if she'd always belonged there. "I can't believe I have to leave tomorrow," she said.

"I wanted to talk to you about that," he said.

"I have to leave," she said.

"No. You said you had to be back by Monday. What

if we take another day and fly back early Monday morning? We can fly right into Lexington and I'll have a car there to drive you to the farm. You could be in your office by nine, guaranteed."

"Really?"

Derek nodded. "Stay just one more day."

"All right," Tess said. "One more day."

Derek had wished for a lot of things in the course of his lifetime, but he'd never really wanted anything as badly as he'd wanted Tess to say yes. A lot could happen in one day. After all, his whole life had already changed in the course of twenty-four hours.

7

THE BEACH ON ANGEL CAY sparkled in the sunlight, the white sand reflecting the sun's rays. Tess walked along the water's edge, wearing Derek's cotton shirt knotted loosely around her waist, and the thong bottom from her blue bikini.

Derek was asleep on the chaise beneath a wide beach umbrella, dozing off after they'd made slow, deliberate love beneath the midday sun. As it had been every time they touched, it was more wonderful than the last.

Tess watched as the waves washed up on shore, revealing tiny shells buried in the sand. He'd taught her the names that morning, showing her whelks and periwinkles and conches. She found a perfect strombus with brown and white spots and rinsed it off in the water before dropping it into a plastic cup.

Though Tess knew the memories of her time on the island would last forever, she still needed something to remind her. She'd stolen Derek's bottle of suntan lotion and hidden it in a bag of things she'd take home with her—the water-stained garnet dress she'd worn the night she met Derek, the pretty blue dress he'd bought her for New Year's Eve, and now these shells.

She wanted to pack Derek into the bag and take him home as well. If only life were so simple. Though she'd avoided all talk of a future with him, as time was ticking down, Tess realized she didn't want to live without him. Yet, try as she might, she couldn't picture him on a farm in Kentucky, enduring the boredom and sameness of each day, tied down to an existence that he'd never want.

There was no realistic way to make things work, making the choice between one world or the other. Most women would probably jump at the chance to live in his life, Tess mused. But she could never trust herself to make that choice. After the disaster with Jeffrey, how could she know her true motives?

Life with Derek would be easy. All her problems would magically disappear. There would be no job to worry about, no problems she couldn't solve. She could provide for her father, maybe even buy him a small farm of his own. Yet, how could she survive if that life were ever taken from her?

She'd said it to Derek. It was better not to dream at all than to have to face disappointment. "I've got to be practical," Tess whispered.

She turned and started back toward Derek. There was another option. They could continue on as they were right now, with occasional vacations together, three-day weekends filled with sun and sex. And then they could go back to living their regular lives.

The more Tess thought about that plan, the more she began to believe it was the only possibility. But as her gaze fixed on Derek's naked body, she slowed her pace, doubts creeping in again.

This had been a fantasy for both of them. They'd run away together without any expectations beyond a few days spent in paradise. And now she wanted to ask for more. Though she might have been a wonderful vacation companion and an exciting partner in bed, Tess really didn't have a lot more to offer him.

A sudden realization hit her and the cup of shells slipped from her fingers and spilled onto the sand at her feet. This was no different than what had happened with Jeffrey. She'd been seriously out of her league from the moment she'd met him, and the same could be said for Derek.

Tess ran her hands through her hair and cursed silently. What had she done? She'd promised herself this was all just a fantasy. But somewhere over the past two days she'd begun caring for Derek, feelings that were deep and very real.

She moved to the chaise and watched him sleep, his arm thrown over his head and his hair rumpled. When she was with Derek, she was a much better version of herself. She was happy and carefree. She laughed and loved without hesitation.

Resting her knee on the chaise, she leaned over him

and brushed a kiss across his mouth. He opened his eyes and growled softly. "I fell asleep," he murmured.

Tess nodded. "I guess I wore you out."

Rolling to his side, he grabbed her and pulled her down next to him. "I don't want to waste our last day together sleeping," he said.

"Did you call for the plane?"

"Yeah. Jeremy is flying in this afternoon. He's going to stay at the resort to give us our privacy. We'll leave at sunrise tomorrow."

"I've had such a good time," she said, brushing his hair back from his handsome face.

"Me, too," he said. "Tell me we're going to do this again. That's all I want to hear right now."

"I've been thinking about that," Tess said. "But our lives are just so different."

"How can you say that? We're wonderful together."

"Sure. Here, in this fantasy world, where neither one of us has to worry about a thing."

"Then let's stay here. Let's stay on this island and see where all this goes."

"I have responsibilities," Tess said. "My dad…he counts on me to keep things together."

"We'll bring him down here," Derek said.

"He'd go crazy. The only thing that keeps him from drinking his life away is working with horses. He has to have something to occupy his time."

"Then I'll buy him some horses," Derek said.

Tess sat up, wrapping her arms around her knees

and staring out at the horizon. "Money can't fix every problem."

He reached out and stroked her arm. "It can help." Derek drew a deep breath. "Tell me what you want, Tess. I'll do whatever you want, as long as I can see you again."

"I don't want to make the same mistake twice."

"What? Do you think I'm like Jeffrey? Do you think I'm going to go out there and find another woman the minute you leave?"

"I don't even know if you already have another woman," she said.

"Damn it, Tess, you know me."

"I don't. That's the problem," she cried. "I know the person who's been on this island with me for the past three days, but I have no idea who you are in the real world."

"Then take some time and find out," he said. "Don't write this off just because you're scared you might get hurt. How do you think I feel? I watched you shut Jeffrey out in the course of a day. How do you think that makes me feel about my chances with you?"

"That's completely different," she said.

"How?"

"I didn't love him," Tess said. A long silence hung between them and the next logical step in the conversation. Yet, she couldn't say it. Maybe she'd been swept into all these unfamiliar emotions, but was it love?

"Can't we please figure this out later?" Tess asked. "I just want to have a good time."

He kissed her, lingering over her lips before he nodded. "What do you want to do on your last afternoon here?"

"I just want to be here with you," Tess said. "Just like this."

And that's what they did. They lay next to each other for a long time, just kissing and touching, communicating their affection without using words. This was the way Tess liked it the best, when they didn't have to worry about what came next.

"I can't imagine what my life would have been like if we'd never met," Derek said.

"You would have been stuck in the elevator by yourself, getting drunk on scotch."

"And I would have gone to bed that night, alone, and gotten up the next morning and flown to Seattle and then to San Diego." He smoothed his hand along her thigh, pulling her closer. "What about you? What would have happened if you'd missed that elevator?"

"First, I would have been humiliated. And then I would have gone home and tried to figure out what I was going to do. Then, I probably would have pushed aside my anger and gone back to work."

"No," Derek said. "You would have stayed at the farm? After what Jeffrey did to you?"

"Until I met you, I was very practical," she said.

"And now?"

"Now I think going to make some changes in my life."

"New Year's resolutions?" he asked.

"Yes. A few. I've decided that I'm not going to allow myself to settle anymore. I'm not going to let my fears determine my future." She drew a deep breath. "And I'm going to quit my job."

He stared at her for a long time, then nodded. "I was hoping you'd do that. I don't want you anywhere near that guy. So what are you going to do?"

Tess shrugged. "I have no idea. Find a new job. I'm a good manager. Someone will want to give me a chance."

"I'm going to quit my job, too," Derek said. "I need a change."

"You can't quit. You have a wonderful job."

"I have an awful job," he said. "I spend my life living out of hotel rooms. Flying from place to place. I have no friends. I don't even have a home. I made my New Year's resolution. I am going to settle…down. I'm going to find a place to live, maybe buy a house."

"Where?"

"I don't know. I haven't decided yet. Somewhere in the country. So that when you come to visit, we can run around without our clothes."

Tess laughed. "That has become a thing with us, hasn't it. It's going to be a challenge to remember to put clothes on from now on."

"I have a feeling this year is going to be a lot better than the last." Derek reached down and took her hand, pressing her fingers to his lips. "Are you hungry?"

"For you? Or for food?"

He kissed her mouth. "Food first, then me. I had the resort bring over lunch. It's in the kitchen."

"I'm starving," she said. "Please tell me you ordered some of that pasta I had yesterday."

Derek crawled off the chaise and pulled her to her feet. "Of course I did. I know how to make my lady happy."

Tess glanced over at him as they walked back to the house, their hands linked. For now, it was all right to be his lady. In truth, it felt good. And maybe, for the rest of the day and night, it wouldn't hurt to imagine that they were a couple.

THE BREEZE HAD PICKED UP and a storm was brewing. Derek stood on the beach, watching as lightning illuminated the high-topped clouds and the white-capped waves. The weather fit his mood—restless, brooding, frustrated. He wished for a hurricane, something that would ground their plane and force them to stay on the island for another day. But Derek had accepted the fact that nothing would keep her here with him.

He and Tess had spent their last day together avoiding the inevitable, any discussion of what might happen between them after they left the island. They'd dined on take-out from the resort's restaurant, played on the beach, taken a ride around the island in the Range Rover and finally tumbled into bed. She'd fallen asleep after they'd made love, but Derek had been restless, unable to relax.

There were so many things he wanted to say to her.

He'd always been careful about leading women on, allowing them to believe in something that just wasn't there. Now that he did have feelings, he wasn't quite sure how to express them.

God, he was pathetic. How many impossible business deals had he made in the past five years? Each one had taken every ounce of his persuasive powers to complete, but he'd done it. If he could just apply those same principles to winning Tess's heart, maybe he'd have a chance.

The first step was to determine what she wanted. It was clear she enjoyed their physical relationship. And they got along outside the bedroom as well. But Tess Robertson was fiercely independent and the one thing he could offer her—financial security—didn't seem to interest her at all.

She'd been ready to cede that responsibility to Jeffrey, only to be deceived and betrayed. So he'd always be fighting an uphill battle at best. He just had to prove his feelings for her were real and unwavering, that his motives were pure, and that she could trust him to always protect her. If she wanted to live a simple life, without any of the luxuries they enjoyed on the island, then he was willing to try.

The wind picked up, whipping sand around his feet. He turned away and walked back up to the house. The sun would be coming up in a few hours and then they'd be on their way back to the States. They'd have to go through customs and immigration at the Cincinnati airport, then fly into Lexington. He'd hired a car to take her home from there.

All the plans were in place to end this fantasy. As he looked back over the past few days, he wondered why he hadn't paid closer attention. Time had slipped by so fast, like water through his fingers.

He stared across the courtyard, then stopped short. Tess stood on the verandah outside her room. She wore his cotton shirt, the gauzy fabric blowing in the breeze, her hair tangling around her face. She was the most beautiful creature he'd ever seen in his life.

A selfish man would want to possess her, but Derek just wanted to exist in her orbit. That was enough for him.

She hadn't seen him yet and he took a step back into the shadows, hoping to watch her without being noticed. But his movement caught her attention and she braced her hands on the rail and stared at him. For a long time they stood, absolutely still, as if time had suddenly stopped.

Derek's fingers twitched. He had to touch her, had to hold her. He crossed the courtyard, the tile cool on his bare feet. And when he was beneath her, he looked up, hoping that she needed him as much as he needed her. With a trembling hand, she reached out for him, walking along the length of the verandah until she reached the stairs.

They met halfway. She threw her arms around his neck and their lips met, the kiss filled with uncontrollable need. But her mouth wasn't enough to satisfy him and Derek ran his hands over her body, pushing aside the shirt to touch her sun-kissed skin.

Her hands smoothed over his chest and then moved lower, her fingers brushing along his growing erection. Derek groaned as she began to stroke him through the soft fabric of his board shorts.

Thunder rumbled as the storm moved closer to the island and they stumbled up the stairs. Derek pressed her back against the stucco wall, pulling her leg up alongside his hip. Tess arched against him, the fabric of his shorts causing a delicious friction.

He could wait, the urge to connect overwhelming any thought of a proper seduction. Tess tugged at the tie at the front of his shorts and when it was undone, freed him to her touch. Her fingers wrapped around his shaft and she slowly stroked it. And when he thought he couldn't take any more, she slowly slid down along his body and teased him with her lips and tongue.

Derek's fingers tangled in her hair. He closed his eyes, surrendering to the sensations that her mouth created, currents of desire snaking through his body. This was all he needed in life to survive. Every nerve in his body felt alive and every synapse in his brain crackled with stimulation.

Though his pleasure was almost too intense to bear, Derek didn't surrender. Instead, he let himself dance closer and closer to the edge. When he'd finally had enough, he gently pulled her to her feet and kissed her again, aching to bury himself deep inside of her.

It had started to rain, a soft, warm rain that blew

onto the verandah with every gust of wind. Against the house, they were protected, yet it felt as if they stood in the middle of a raging cyclone of emotions.

Derek picked Tess up and wrapped her legs around his waist, ready to carry her inside to the bed. But this time, Tess couldn't wait. She gently guided him inside her. The feel of her body surrounding him, without any barriers between them, was exquisite torture.

"Are you sure?" he whispered.

Tess sighed as she pulled away, then sank down onto his shaft again. "Don't worry."

Though Derek suspected that she was safe from pregnancy, he wasn't certain. And yet, he didn't really care. He had every intention of being a part of her future. Whatever might happen wouldn't change how he felt about her. He'd fallen in love with Tess and there was no going back.

He pressed her back against the wall with every thrust. And as he increased his pace, he felt her need rising right along with his. She whispered his name again and again, the frantic rhythm of her words matching that of his body's movements.

A soft cry tore from her throat and then she dissolved into spasms of release. Her orgasm took him by surprise, her cries of pleasure mingling with the sounds of the storm. The feel of her body melting into his was just enough to shatter his self-control. Derek drove into her one last time and then surrendered, his own release turning his limbs weak and his mind hazy.

They stood against the wall for a long time, waiting

for their breathing to return to normal. Derek buried his face in the curve of her neck. He fought the urge to tell her everything he felt. This wasn't the end of what they'd shared, but only the beginning.

Yet, every instinct told him to move slowly, to give her time. Tess wasn't ready to trust. For now, he would have to be satisfied with whatever she was willing to give, whether it be her body, her heart or her entire soul.

"I think I better get off my feet before I fall down," he whispered.

Holding tight to her, Derek carried her inside and gently laid her down on the bed, stretching out beside her. As they lay together, he began to move again, very slowly. "I could live like this," he said.

"How?"

"Lying beside you every night, waking up with you every morning."

"It is a nice fantasy," she said, wrapping her legs around his waist. Tess smiled then smoothed her hand over his cheek. "And I will miss this."

THE SMALL JET GLIDED through the early-morning sky, its engines rumbling softly. To the east, the reds and oranges of the sunrise were visible through the windows. Tess sat across from Derek, curled up in the wide leather seat. She knew she had to put some distance between them before they actually had to say their goodbyes. For now, physical distance was all she could manage.

She could feel him watching her, waiting for her to

start a conversation about what was about to happen. Tess had so much to say to him, yet he didn't seem to want to hear any of it. All he wanted was another day together, another two days. And she couldn't give that to him.

They'd land in Cincinnati in less than an hour, then would fly on to Lexington. Derek had hired a car to take her home to the farm. At first, he'd insisted on accompanying her to the farm just to make sure she got home safely, but Tess knew it would only make their goodbyes more difficult. She'd stubbornly refused his offer, preferring to say their farewells at the Lexington airport.

They'd had a wonderful time together. And as the days passed, she'd realized that she deserved something better than what Jeffrey had offered her. Though she hoped there might come a time for her to fall in love, Tess couldn't allow herself to feel that way about Derek.

She'd never really know her true motives for choosing to be with him. Love was so easy to confuse with need. In their time together, she'd learned so many of his intimate secrets, the perfect places to touch him and to kiss him. And he knew all the ways to make her writhe with pleasure and beg for release. But pure desire would never be enough to sustain them in the long run.

They'd gone about this all wrong, backward. She knew his body, but still didn't know the most basic things about him—where he'd gone to college, his favorite color, his musical tastes? All of these things were important facts to learn, but they had simply run out of time. "Where did you go to college?" Tess asked.

He turned and looked at her as if startled that she'd spoken. "What?"

"College? Where did you go?"

"Columbia," he said. "In New York City. And then Yale for grad school. What about you?"

"University of Kentucky. In Lexington."

"Okay," he murmured. "Good." Derek paused. "And what did you major in?"

"Equine science and management," she said. "Why?"

"Just curious," he said. "What is your dad's name?"

"George Robertson."

"And the farm you live on?"

"Beresford Farms," she replied, frowning. "We really don't know anything about each other, do we?"

Derek shrugged. "No, I guess not. But is any of that stuff really important?"

"Maybe not, but it is a part of who we are."

Derek pushed out of his seat and sat down next to her, twisting around so he could face her. "I know it seems like we're still strangers in a lot of ways," he said, taking her hands in his. "And the farther we get from the island, the farther apart we seem to be."

"I know," Tess said.

"We've gotten closer in three days than I've been to a woman in my entire life. When I'm with you, I feel as if I've known you for years."

"Getting to know each other takes time. Only we didn't have a lot of time."

"We have another hour," he said. "Ask me anything. And tell me everything. I want to fill in all the blanks. You've told me your dreams, now tell me your fears."

"We could just kiss for the last hour," she suggested. The last thing she wanted to do was talk, but the intent look on Derek's face told her he wasn't giving her a choice. She drew a ragged breath. "There were times, long periods of time, when we were technically...homeless. We lived out of my dad's truck. We'd drive all over the country, from farm to farm, looking for work. Then there were times when we'd make enough money for a motel room or gas money, but my dad would take it and drink it away or gamble it at the track."

Derek reached out and took her hand, drawing it to his lips to kiss it. He didn't say anything, as if he sensed there were no words to wash away the memories of that time, especially coming from someone like him.

"Some nights, my dad would go out to a bar and I'd lock myself in the truck and pull a blanket over my head and hope that no one would come along and bother me. Then, we'd go from that to living on a farm where the owners spent more on a new horse trailer than we could ever hope to make in five years. The horses were worth more than we were."

"Tess, I—"

"I'm not complaining," she interrupted. "It made me strong. And things are better now. I have job skills and a good résumé. Lots of people have sad stories to tell, Derek. And a lot of them say that money can't buy happiness. So who knows how much better our lives might have been had we been swimming in cash?"

"It could have helped," he said.

Tess shrugged. "I remember how I felt, all alone in that truck. I used to think, if I only had a real home, I'd do everything in my power to keep it. I was going to marry Jeffrey to do just that. But then you swept me away. And I think it was probably the best thing that could have happened to me."

He slipped his arm around her shoulders and pulled her into his lap. "You never have to worry," he whispered. "If you need anything, you know you can come to me."

The rest of the trip home went so quickly. They'd talked about everything inconsequential and nothing important, but by the time they landed in Lexington, Tess felt as if they did know each other better—at least the facts that made up their lives.

Before she knew it, they were standing on the tarmac, outside a small hangar in a remote part of the Lexington airport, a black town car waiting to whisk her back to reality.

Tess stood in front of Derek, her feet suddenly frozen in place. She'd thought it would be easy to walk away from the fantasy. But this was no longer a dream—it was her life and she didn't want to let it go. Tess couldn't shake the feeling that this might be the last time she ever saw him.

Could it be more difficult? Every shred of common sense she possessed told her to think practically. They came from different worlds. And though a weekend spent in Derek's world was a fantasy come true, living in a fantasy world full-time wasn't a good idea for someone like her.

She'd fought so hard to get where she was. Against all odds, she gotten an education and held a great job. And she was good at that job. No, not just good—great. Could she risk all that on a gamble that he'd love her for the rest of her life?

She'd been happy with her life the way it was, satisfied with what her job provided. And now, in one weekend, that had all been undone. No matter what happened between her and Derek, her real life would never quite measure up again.

Being lost in a fantasy for three whole days had changed her, had somehow altered her so deeply that she wasn't the same person anymore. But was she unhappy because she was losing the creature comforts that Derek could provide? Or was she unhappy because she was losing Derek?

"If we stand here all night, your plane is going to run out of gas," Tess murmured.

He gathered her into his arms and gave her a hug. "I'll buy more gas. I don't want to let you go. Not yet."

"It won't be such a big deal if we just say goodbye and walk away," she said. She'd done it so many times in her life, with the few childhood friends she'd made along the way. One minute she was there and the next, the truck would be packed and they'd be on their way again. It wasn't so hard if it was done quickly—like ripping off a bandage or pulling out a loose tooth.

"I told the driver to text me after he's delivered you safely," he said. "But you can always call and let me know you got home all right."

She nodded.

"I don't want to pressure you, Tess. I don't want to ask you to do anything you don't want to do or make any promises you can't keep. What I *do* want is to see you again. So here's my plan. I won't call, I won't text or email. But I will send the jet to pick you up exactly two weeks from this coming Friday. It will be waiting, right here in this spot at 6:00 p.m. And if you want to continue on with this, get on the jet and come to me."

"What if I can't? I'm probably going to be looking for work."

"I'll be waiting."

She stared at him for a long time. "And if I don't show up?"

"Then I'll assume it's over," he said. "And I won't try to change your mind. I'll respect your decision."

She could live with that. Things would be so much clearer once she'd stepped away from all that had happened to her over the weekend. She needed a good dose of reality to get her feet back beneath her. Once she could put some perspective on it all, then maybe she could figure out how she really felt about Derek.

He stared down at her, his gaze flitting over her face. "All right," he said. "I'm going to turn around and get in the plane and you're going to turn around and get in the car. We'll go our separate ways."

"Yes," she said.

"No," Derek replied. "I'm going to stand here and watch you drive away. I'm not getting on the plane until you're gone. And then I'm going to wait ten or fifteen minutes just to make sure you haven't changed your mind and decided to come back."

"I'm not going to change my mind," she said.

"You have your fantasies, let me have mine," he said with a smile.

"All right," Tess said. "So, kiss me once more. And make it good."

Derek hooked his thumb under her chin and tipped her mouth up to meet his. Their lips met, softly at first. His hands skimmed over her body, trying to imagine the soft flesh beneath her clothes. Her head swam with images of them together, limbs tangled, naked bodies intimately joined.

And when he finally drew back, Tess's heart was slamming in her chest and she found it difficult to draw a breath. She ached to think about not having him near, a deep, searing pain that seemed to surround her heart.

"Goodbye, Derek," she murmured, her eyes still closed.

"Goodbye, Tess."

She turned away from him without opening her eyes, then began to walk to the car. The driver stood by the rear door.

"Tess!"

She stopped, but didn't turn around. She didn't want to look at him for fear that she'd dissolve into tears and go running back to him. "I think I'm in love with you, Tess. I just thought you should know that. In fact, I'm pretty sure I'm in love with you. Ninety-nine percent sure. Maybe closer to a hundred percent."

Tess turned around and faced him. Her eyes were swimming with tears and a tiny smile touched the corners of her mouth. She raised her hand and waved, then got into the car.

8

THE CAR DOOR CLOSED and Derek took a deep breath for the first time since they'd stepped off the plane. He'd said it—what he'd been thinking for the past day or two but was afraid to admit. For now, that would have to be enough.

As promised, he watched her until the car disappeared from view and then waited another fifteen minutes. Jeremy joined him on the tarmac, staring off into the distance with him.

"So, are we going to take off, or are you going to stand out here all day?"

"I'm going to stand here for a little while longer," Derek said.

"You really think she might come back?"

"I can hope, can't I?" Derek glanced over at Jeremy. "I told her how I felt. That might make a difference. It always does in the movies." At his confused expression, Derek continued. "You know, the heroine leaves and the hero stands there like his world has just come to an end. And then she comes back and throws herself into his arms and they kiss."

"Oh, yeah. And he twirls her around. That's the end of every chick movie I've ever seen. I prefer when the hero pulls her out of burning wreckage and they walk off into the sunset."

"Either way would work for me," Derek said.

"You told her you loved her." Jeremy sighed. "That's big, man. I mean, that usually does the trick. Unless she doesn't believe you."

"It feels good. I haven't said those words in five years. And back then, I didn't have a clue what I was saying. Now I know."

"I guess that's all you can ask for," Jeremy said. "So you think she's the one?"

Derek nodded. "Yeah. She's the one."

"If she's the one, why didn't you follow her? Instead of standing here waiting for her to come back, you should have gone after her."

"No, I don't think she's ready for that. I'm just going to give her a little time to figure out what she wants."

His thoughts wandered back over the events of that weekend—the long, lazy nights in bed, the days spent lying in the sun. It was difficult to believe that it was little more than three days since they'd met in that elevator.

"Where to, boss?" Jeremy asked.

"I don't know. I don't think I want to go to work.

And before I take off, I need to messenger something to Tess."

"Why didn't you just give it to her?" Jeremy asked.

He reached into his pocket and withdrew an envelope containing a check for $34,000, her winnings from the casino. She'd refused to take the money from him and at the time, he hadn't wanted to fight about it. But Derek knew he'd feel better if Tess had access to the funds. "She wouldn't have taken it. And I didn't want to give her the choice."

Derek handed him the envelope with Tess's address scrawled on the front. "Take this along when you file your flight plan and have them messenger it to her. Put the charges on your company card. Then let's get out of here."

"I need to know where we're going before I can file a flight plan," Jeremy said.

"Virginia," Derek said. "I want to go to Virginia. Just pick an airport and we'll go from there."

"You don't have any hotels in Virginia," Jeremy said.

"Yeah. I know. I just want to check it out, maybe look at a few farms."

"Why would you be looking at farms?"

Derek chuckled. "I'm thinking it's about time I put down roots. And Virginia sounds like a nice place to settle."

Derek walked back to the plane. While Jeremy took care of business, he got out his cell phone and made a few calls. It was strange how his life had been on one single track for such a long time and now, in the course of a few days, he was jumping the rails and headed in a different direction.

There was an excitement in the prospect of shaking things up. Though he wasn't sure where he'd end up, he knew he didn't want to go back to where he had been— alone…without Tess.

He brought out his laptop and did a quick search for horse farms in Virginia, bookmarking the farms he wanted to see. Though he didn't know a thing about raising horses or what was required to house them, Derek figured buying a farm would be the most sensible choice, especially if he wanted to convince Tess he wanted a future with her.

He sank back in the leather seat and clicked through a set of photos of a property in northern Virginia, about ninety minutes outside Washington, D.C. He'd lived his adult life in cities, but he could imagine himself spending time in the country. All he needed was an airstrip nearby that could accommodate the Lear jet and he'd be fine.

As he read the details of the property, Derek tried to find qualities that might appeal to Tess. A swimming pool would be nice. She loved the courtyard garden at Angel Cay and the wide verandahs. Hell, he wouldn't even have to buy an existing property. He could build her a farm from the ground up.

Jeremy stepped back into the plane and pulled the door closed. "We're all set. We're flying into Richmond.

I know a place there that serves the best biscuits and gravy."

"Sounds good. I'm ready to go."

Derek got up and walked to the cockpit, strapping himself into the copilot's seat. As the plane raced down the runway and took flight, he looked down at the gray landscape below.

Somewhere, on one of those roads, Tess was making her way back to her real life. Loneliness ached inside him as the distance between them grew. But he'd be back. When he returned, he and Tess would begin where they left off. And sooner or later, there would come a time when they wouldn't have to leave each other again. They'd find a place where they could be together for good.

Tess stood at the stable door, an invoice in her hand. "Did you check the order when it came in?" she asked.

"Yeah," her father shouted. "They were short six bags of the vitamin mix. I called and they said they'd send it on the next order and they did."

"But they billed it twice," she shouted.

George Robertson stepped out of the stall, leading the thoroughbred filly. He was dressed in faded denim, a plaid shirt and riding boots. He was a small, wiry man, all sinewy muscle and not an ounce of fat. Though he was only in his early fifties, years of drinking and working in the sun made him look a lot older.

"Look at her. Isn't she a beaut? When they walked

her off the trailer, she looked right at me and I swear, she smiled. It's a sign. This horse is going to win some races."

"Daddy, if you're going to sign for orders, you have to be more careful. Or just let Jimmy sign for them. He knows what he's doing."

"I know what the hell I'm doing," her father grumbled. "What's so hard?" He patted the filly on her flank. "Look at her, Tessie. She's the one. I can feel it in my bones. I gotta get her ready. Mr. Jeffrey and Mr. Frank are coming to take a good look at her. I'm going to have Jack put her through her paces." Her father nervously fiddled with the halter on the horse. "She looks good, doesn't she? You think she looks good?"

"Daddy, don't worry. They're no better than you and they certainly don't know more about horses than you. Just tell them what you see."

"That is not a good attitude."

"Well, maybe I don't hold such a high opinion of the Beales anymore."

"Word is Mr. Jeffrey got engaged. They were talking about it in the kitchen last night." He rubbed his stubbly chin. "I wonder if he'll bring her along?"

"Oh, I don't think that's going to happen," Tess said. Jeffrey would have to be crazy to bring his new fiancée to the farm. Was he that narcissistic that he didn't expect any blowback from his announcement? She intended to let him know exactly what she thought of him at the first available opportunity.

Tess turned and walked back to her office in the

east stable. She'd already decided to quit, but she hadn't determined exactly how she'd do it. She could begin making inquiries, maybe take the time to find a suitable place for them, and then resign at Beresford Farms. She suspected her meeting with Jeffrey would determine her course of action.

But where would they go? California? Saratoga? They'd worked in Florida a few times and she'd enjoyed the warm weather. She'd sit down after work and make a list of contacts she could call. Her reputation as a good manager was well-known and they'd spent nearly ten years at Beresford. Their prospects were much better than they'd ever been before.

Tess flipped through the invoices as she walked through the stable and opened the door to her office. She was about to sit down at her desk when she heard his voice. "Hello, Tess."

Tess sucked in a sharp breath and looked up to find Jeffrey lounging on the leather sofa in the corner, his legs crossed casually in front of him. She stared at him for a long moment, wondering what she'd ever seen in him. He was charming enough. And he had an easy confidence. But all she could feel for him was mild disgust.

He slowly stood, holding out his hands. "Listen, I want to apologize. I know I should have told you what was going on, but I—"

"You invited me to your engagement party," she said, her voice tight. "What were you thinking?"

"My parents invited you. I didn't know until I got

upstairs. Once I found out, I meant to talk to you before the party and explain. But when you didn't show up, I figured you'd heard."

"Yeah, I heard."

"Come on, Tess, don't be mad. I thought we were on the same page. You never mentioned marriage. You seemed happy with the way things were."

"We never talked! How do you know what I wanted?"

"Whose fault is that? But I want you to know, this engagement doesn't change how I feel about you. I like you, Tess, and I want to continue liking you."

"Oh, well, that makes me feel so much better."

"We can continue on as we have. There's no reason to stop seeing each other."

"You're engaged to someone else," she said, shaking her head. "How could you think that I'd find that even remotely acceptable?" She drew a deep breath. "I don't want you ever talking to me again. I'm resigning my position. I'll pack my things and be out of here by the end of the week. Until then, I want you to stay the hell away from me or I'll call your fiancée and tell her what went on between us."

He took a step forward. "Is that a threat?"

"Take it any way you want. As long as we stay out of each other's way, you'll be fine."

"Tess, this isn't necessary," Jeffrey said. "You don't have to leave. No one wants you to go."

Tess crossed the office, coming toe-to-toe with him. "I want to go." He reached out to touch her arm, but she slapped him away. "I'll leave it to you to explain this to your father. And when the time comes, I'll expect you to give me a glowing recommendation." She shook her head. "I must have been blind or completely stupid to have ever thought you were worth my time. And someday your fiancée, or your wife, will find out exactly who and what you are. Charm will only take you so far, Jeffrey. Time to grow up."

He smiled, then shrugged. "Well, I'm sure you'll find a good situation, Tess. Good luck to you both. And if you ever change your mind, just give me a call."

He walked out of the office, closing the door behind him. Tess picked up a stapler from her desktop and hurled it at the door. "I'm never going to change my mind!" It hit the wall with a thud, then dropped to the floor. "Stupid," she muttered. "Idiot."

Tess sat down at her desk and buried her face in her hands. She waited for the fear to set in, that old feeling that always came whenever her life took a sudden nosedive. But as her temper cooled, Tess realized she wasn't afraid. In fact, she was excited. The thought of taking complete control of her destiny gave her a wonderful sense of power. She had enough cash in the bank to cover about two months of job searching. And, if that wasn't enough, she had a few credit cards she could max out if she had to.

She picked up her cell phone and looked at the screen, fighting the urge to call Derek. He was probably in the air, on his way to some exotic location. But she wanted to tell him of her decision, to find out his opinion on it all, to just hear his deep, rich voice saying her name.

Her cell phone rang and she looked at the caller ID. Tess let out a tightly held breath, then answered the call. "I'm back, I'm back," she said. "I'm sorry, I was supposed to call, I know."

"You were," Alison said in a scolding tone. "You don't know how worried I've been. I tried calling you and I—"

"My phone died and I didn't have my charger with me. I literally just walked into the office an hour ago and plugged it in."

"So, tell me all about your weekend."

"Can we talk about this another time?" Tess asked. "I'm in the middle of a little crisis here."

"What's wrong? Horse problems?"

"Job problems. I just quit. And I haven't told my father yet."

Alison gasped. "Tess. Wow, I don't know what to say. Good for you."

"Really? You think it's a good idea? I'd been thinking I could probably suck it up and stay until I found another job, then quit. But then Jeffrey stopped by and actually suggested that we continue our relationship."

"What a snake," Alison said. "I knew there was a reason I didn't like him. How do you think your dad will take this?"

"He likes it here. This is the closest thing we've had to a home. We've been here ten years. I was seventeen when we moved in. I followed him for all those years and now I'm going to have to ask him to follow me."

"Where are you going to go? Do you know?"

"Nope."

"What about Derek? How did you leave things with him?"

"He wants to see me again. He's sending the plane the weekend after next and if I want to see him, I'm supposed go. But I've got to get my own life straightened out before I can figure out what's going on with him." Tess paused. "That sounded good, didn't it?"

"But it's not the truth?"

Tess sighed. "It should be. But I can't stop thinking of everything that happened on that island. Oh, Ali, it was so incredible. Like an unending fantasy that just kept getting better and better."

"And how do you feel about him?"

"I think I could fall in love with him. But I'm afraid to, afraid I'm falling for some fantasy. Everything with him is just so perfect. But nothing is that perfect in the real world."

"Where are you going to go?"

"I don't know. But I've been kind of toying with the idea of buying a small farm. I don't know how much money it would take or if I could even get a loan, but it's one option I'd like to consider."

A knock sounded on Tess's office door and she looked up to see a strange man standing on the other side. She waved him inside. "Listen, I'm going to have to call you back. I've got someone here right now."

Tess said goodbye to Alison just as a young man in a blue uniform stepped inside. "Tess Robertson?"

"That's me."

"I have a delivery for you." He handed her a clipboard and she signed in her name before taking the envelope from his hand. "Have a nice day."

Tess waited until he left, then examined the envelope carefully. She was almost afraid to open it. Was Jeffrey about to pull some kind of legal maneuver on her? It would be just like him to force her to stay. Cursing softly, she tore open the envelope and withdrew a check.

"Oh," she murmured, immediately recognizing what it was. Her winnings from the casino. Derek had found a way to make her take the money, giving her no chance to argue. She stared at the check, running her fingers over her name typed on it. It was more than enough for a down payment on a farm. And all that was standing in her way was her pride.

She folded the check in half and shoved it in the back pocket of her jeans. Though she wasn't sure she'd cash it, it gave her a boost of courage to know it was there—in case of emergency.

As Tess walked out of her office, she smiled to herself. He hadn't ridden to her rescue, but Derek knew what she'd be going through and he'd known exactly how to make her feel better. Even from a distance, he'd discovered a way to make her happy.

Tess found her father in a stall, bent over a horse's hoof and cleaning it with a pick. "Daddy?"

He looked up, then struggled to his feet. Every year it was harder and harder for him to do the manual labor. His knees ached and his hands were plagued with arthritis. "They like the filly," he said. "They think she looks real good. I told you. It's a sign."

"Come out here and sit down. I need to talk to you about something."

"What's wrong? I can tell from the way you look. I didn't mean to mess up that order. It's just that I was busy with other things and maybe I didn't count and—"

"It's not that." She drew a deep breath. "Daddy, I just quit."

Her father's expression fell—and Tess's heart broke into a thousand pieces. She hadn't seen him look like that in years. She'd hoped she'd never have to see it again. "It's not your fault," she said. "It's mine. I just think it's time to move on. And I'd like you to go with me."

"Of course, Tessie. We're a team. But where are we going to go?"

"I was thinking, maybe we could buy a little farm of our own? I've saved some money. I think we might be able to scrape together a down payment. It won't be a fancy place like this. Just a small one. But it would be ours."

It had always been her father's dream to have his own farm to run. "We might be able to find a few investors," he said. "I've got some contacts. And with the two of us working together, I know we could make a go of it."

"We can think about that if we need to," she said.

"It'll be just the two of us again," he said. "Like the old days," her father said. "Remember that, Tessie? Living out of the back of our pickup truck. It was a good life back then, wasn't it? We didn't have any strings tying us down. No bosses telling us what to do."

"Yeah, Daddy, it was a really good life," she said softly.

"How much longer do you think we'll wait?" Jeremy asked.

Derek turned away from the window. "Are you in a hurry?"

"This freezing rain could give us some icing problems. If we don't leave within the next hour, we might be stuck here until we can deice."

Derek glanced at his watch. Maybe he'd been a bit optimistic to believe Tess would be waiting for him when he arrived. They hadn't spoken in two weeks—not that he hadn't wanted to call. Hell, he'd spent the past fourteen days thinking about her, planning exactly what he wanted to say to her, the words he'd use to convince her they belonged together.

And now that the time had come, it appeared he might not have the chance. She was already forty-five minutes late. How much longer would it be before he started to look desperate and pathetic?

"Maybe the roads are icy," Jeremy said. "There are all kinds of reasons she could be delayed."

"No," Derek said. "She has my number. If she was running late, she could have called. She's not coming."

He turned back to the window, staring out into the darkness beyond the private hangar. Maybe it was for the best, he mused. They'd never intended their relationship to be anything more than just a weekend affair. For all he knew, she'd gone home and patched things up with her soon-to-be-married boyfriend. Derek cursed softly. She deserved a whole lot more than playing second fiddle to some society bride.

He had to face the fact that he really didn't know who Tess Robertson was. Sure, he knew what he'd seen on the island, but Derek had no way to determine if that was really the woman she was—or just part of the fantasy. He'd fallen in love with the girl in the elevator. For all he knew, there was a different woman lurking beneath that beautiful facade.

"Hey!"

Derek looked up to find Jeremy standing in the door to the cockpit. "What's up?"

"There's a pickup truck parked out there. It's just sitting on the tarmac. I think it might be your girl."

Derek got out of his seat and strode forward, brushing past Jeremy as he moved into the cockpit. He took the copilot's seat and stared out the window through the icy drizzle. The truck was running, the wipers sliding across the windshield, but the headlights were off.

"How long has it been there?"

"I don't know," Jeremy said. "I just noticed it when I was going through preflight. What are you going to do?"

"I'm going to go see if it's Tess," he said. Derek opened the hatch and waited for the stairs to unfold, then ran through the rain to the waiting pickup. He could see her through the foggy windows and he tapped on the driver's side and waited. Slowly, the window rolled down.

Tess glanced up at him. "Hi," she murmured.

"What are you doing?" Derek asked.

"I don't know. I haven't really decided."

"Okay," Derek said. "So, I'll wait. Just take your time." He turned and leaned against the truck, staring up at the dismal sky. "This is nasty weather."

"Get in," she said.

Smiling, Derek jogged around to the other side of the truck and opened the door. He slid into the passenger seat, then ran his hands through his damp hair. "It's cold out there."

"You're wet," she said, forcing a smile.

"That's what happens when you stand in the rain." He was almost afraid to touch her. She seemed so fragile, so uncertain of what she was doing. Her gaze kept darting over at him, before going back to a spot outside the car. "It's good to see you."

She looked different. Her wavy hair was pulled back and tied with a scarf. She wore a faded denim jacket, a form-fitting T-shirt and a long flowing skirt with leather riding boots. And yet, she was still the same beautiful woman he'd seduced on the island. "How long have you been here?" Derek asked.

"A half hour," she said. "I wasn't going to come, but then I thought you deserved an explanation for why I couldn't come. I was going to call, but that didn't seem to be the right thing to do."

"So, you've decided not to get on the plane with me?" Derek said.

"Yes." She took a deep breath. "Yes, I've decided not to get on the plane. I can't. Not right now."

"Yes, you can. You're perfectly capable of getting out of your truck and walking across that tarmac and stepping onto that plane. You can. You just don't want to."

"But I do. I really, really want to," Tess said. "I want to believe I can go with you and all my problems will be solved and—"

"You're still in love with him, aren't you?" Derek said.

"What?"

"Jeffrey. You're still in love with him."

"No!" she cried as if hurt by his statement. "No, I pretty much hate everything about him. I quit my job. My father and I are living in a cheap motel outside Richmond, Virginia, while I look for work or find a small farm to buy, whichever comes first."

Derek chuckled. "Well, that makes me feel much better. So, why won't you get on the plane?"

"Because it's the easy thing to do," Tess said, her brow furrowed. "And I'm not sure of my reasons for wanting to do it. I've been thinking about you a lot, Derek. And remembering our time on the island. A few days away would be wonderful, but—"

"It doesn't have to be a few days," Derek said. "I'd like to think what we have might last a little longer than that."

"What do we have?" Tess asked.

Derek shook his head. "This isn't how and when I planned to say all this," he said. "And this certainly isn't where, but if it has to be, I can deal with it." He reached out and took her hand. "I meant what I said to you two weeks ago. I'm hopelessly in love with you, Tess. I know that might be a bit surprising and I'm a little shocked myself, but there it is. I want you in my life. I don't care how it happens, but I'm going to make it happen."

"Just like that?"

"Yeah, that's how it works. When I decide on a course of action, I can be tenacious. You can say no, but that's not going to change my mind."

"You said I had a choice," she countered.

"That was then. This is now. Now I'm not giving you a choice. So, if you don't want to get on that plane, then I'll just stay in your truck. We can spend the night here…in the damp…and the cold…freezing our asses off." He sighed, shaking his head. "Or we can be on the beach at Angel Cay in a few hours."

"You're going to have to kidnap me," Tess warned.

"That is an option." He grinned.

Tears of frustration glittered in her eyes and Derek cursed inwardly. He hadn't expected tears and he never wanted to cause her any kind of pain, but he had to prove to her that his feelings were real. "Come on, Tess, just give it a chance. Let me into your life. I promise, I won't hurt you."

"My life," she said. "Right now, I don't know what my life is. I'm still trying to figure that out."

He reached out and grabbed her chin, wiping the tears from her cheeks. "You have me. You'll always have me. Now stop crying."

"I don't have the energy to argue about this."

"Then maybe we should stop arguing and you should kiss me," he said.

Tess gripped the steering wheel. "You're really not going to get out of my car, are you?"

Derek shook his head. "Nope."

"I'm not sure I want to kiss you," she murmured.

He reached over and caught her chin again, turning her to face him. "It's really good to see you, Tess."

She smiled weakly. "It's really good to see you, too," she murmured.

Derek reached out and grabbed her waist, then pulled her on top of him, stretching out on the front seat of the truck. "I've missed having you in my bed," he said, his fingers tangling in her hair. "And it isn't just the sex I missed." Derek kissed her softly. "I like the way you make me feel. I like talking to you and touching you and hearing you laugh. And I don't like seeing you so sad. What can we do about that?"

"You could kiss me again," she whispered.

He gently captured her mouth, his fingers slipping through her hair as he molded her lips to his. The kiss was long and deep and delicious.

She clutched at the front of his shirt and he twisted beneath her, trying to find a comfortable spot for them both. "I can't do this," he murmured.

"What? Why not?"

"We're in a pickup truck!" Derek sat up. "How can anyone get romantic here? We barely have enough room to move."

"Plenty of people get busy in the front seat of a pickup," Tess said. "At least in my world, they do. I had my first sexual encounter in a pickup."

He grinned at her. "I didn't know that."

"There are a lot of things you still don't know about me."

Derek stared at her pretty face. How could he possibly resist this woman? He'd almost forgotten how much fun they had together, how well they got along. Maybe this was what love was really all about—not passion and desire, but quiet moments in the front of a battered old truck.

Tess moaned softly as he kissed her again. He tugged at her jacket then tossed it on the floor, anxious to find all his favorite spots on her body. When she pulled her T-shirt over her head, Derek's breath caught in his throat. Over the past two weeks, he'd imagined this scene in his head, again and again. But it had never been even close to the real thing.

Grabbing the hem of his shirt, he pulled it over his head, the sound of ripping fabric splitting the silence. The close quarters of the pickup made it nearly impossible to undress. But Derek didn't care.

When he finally entered her, his heart was beating so hard he thought it might explode. Their gazes locked and he began to move, his hands clutching her hips as he drove into her, slowly at first and then with a more determined rhythm.

There had been no foreplay, but Tess didn't seem to care. This was exactly what she wanted from him. "Oh," she moaned when he shifted, his movements causing a wave of pleasure to race through his body. He felt himself dancing on the edge of control and she moved again.

"Oh!" Tess cried. "Oh, that's perfect," she whispered. "Just like that."

Derek watched her, his gaze searching her face and waiting for the telltale signs that she was close to her release. "Now tell me you want me to stop," he teased. "I'll stop. I swear I will."

"No," she said, closing her eyes and tipping her head back. "I never want you to stop."

And when she finally gave herself over to her orgasm, Derek knew he had nothing to worry about. She needed this as much as he did. She found comfort in sex, an escape, a perfect place where she could be herself again. No other man could give that to her.

But Derek wasn't going to let her off the hook so easily. If she wasn't going to come with him, then he had no choice but to force the issue. "So this was nice," he murmured. "We should do it again sometime." He searched the floor for his shirt, then sat up and pulled it over his head.

Tess drew back, her arms clutched in front of her, covering her bare breasts. "Are you just going to leave?"

"You don't want to come with me," Derek said. "And

you don't want me to come with you. I guess we've reached an impasse." He reached out and cupped her cheek in his palm. "I know you love me. Maybe not as much as I love you, but I'm willing to wait. When you're finally ready to admit it, you can give me a call."

"You just can't walk out!" Tess said.

"Yes, I can." He nodded toward the plane. "Actually, I'm going to fly out."

"Wait," Tess said, reaching out to grab his arm. "Just wait."

"What? Tell me, Tess. What do you want?"

He watched her face, praying that she'd finally give in, that she'd finally admit she needed him. But she could only shake her head. "Go," she murmured.

"You're sure?"

Tess nodded, grabbing her T-shirt and yanking it over her head. "Yes."

Derek cursed beneath his breath. "I don't think I've ever met anyone as stubborn as you are. There's no disgrace in admitting how you feel. I love you. I want to make your life as happy as possible. But if you won't let me do that, then we're always going to end up here—going our separate ways."

"I just need some time," she said.

Derek reached out and took her face between his hands, giving her a long, fierce kiss. "Just don't wait too long."

With that, he hopped out of the truck and slammed the door behind him. As he strode across the tarmac, he tucked his shirt into his pants and zipped them up.

He was willing to wait as long as she needed. Tess was worth every lonely hour and then some. But that didn't mean he'd make it easy on her.

When he jogged up the steps to the plane, he found Jeremy waiting just inside. "We've got to go if we're going," he said. "This weather isn't getting any better."

"Go," Derek said.

"You don't want to wait and see if she comes running back?"

"It's not going to happen," he said. "At least, not this time."

9

THE WINDOW OF TESS'S PICKUP was open as she sped along the country road. After a month of chilly February weather, spring was finally in the air. She'd already grown accustomed to her daily trip to the hardware store in town and could almost make the drive with her eyes closed.

They'd found the farm in south central Virginia at the end of January and closed the deal two weeks later. After saving enough for taxes, she'd put the check from her gambling win into the bank and used it for the down payment.

The small farm had been the only place they could afford with enough acreage to raise horses. And though the land was beautiful, the farmhouse was barely habitable. It had been used for feed storage. The rooms were dusty and the windows so caked with grime they barely let in the light.

The barn, however, was in good shape, with well-maintained stalls for sixteen horses. Within a month they'd managed to find six horses to board and exercise and the reputation that Tess had built at Beresford Farms was making it easy to market her services as a management troubleshooter.

She hadn't seen Derek since the night he'd come to pick her up at the Lexington airport. They spoke once every week when he called to ask if she might like to fly down to Angel Cay for the weekend. But with all the work to do to make the house habitable, Tess had been forced to put him off. And then, last night he hadn't called.

She'd begun to feel maybe she'd made a mistake not leaving with him that night. How would her life have been different if she'd gotten on the plane? Maybe he would have convinced her to stay with him. And maybe she wouldn't have bought the farm.

All the doubts she thought she'd conquered had come rushing back. As she sat alone in her heatless, unfurnished, crumbling farmhouse, Tess had wanted Derek there to tell her she hadn't completely screwed up her future.

As she turned west off the main road, Tess slowed to look down the long, tree-lined drive of Ridgedale Farm, the huge horse farm that bordered her own. It was state of the art—everything she'd ever dreamed of. But she was through with dreams. The For Sale sign tacked onto the white paddock fence now had a Sold sign nailed on top of it. Tess made a mental note to call her real estate agent and find out who had bought the farm. Maybe they'd need some help around the place. And with her father working on their farm, she might even be able to take a full-time manager's job.

Her mood brightened. She would make this work. It would be a struggle financially, but she and her father had lived on the edge before. And now that her life was back on track, she and Derek could take some time away.

She reached for her phone, then dropped it back on the front seat of the truck, an uneasy feeling coming over her. Maybe he hadn't called for a reason. Had Derek's patience finally worn thin? Tess drew a ragged breath. Or maybe he'd met another woman, someone he found much more interesting.

Just the thought of someone else spending time with him on their island brought a sick feeling to her stomach. She pushed the thought from her head, stubbornly determined not to let herself get carried away. Tess had already prepared herself for the worst. If he didn't really love her, if all that he'd said was just part of the fantasy and couldn't survive in the real world, then she could understand.

After all, she'd gone into their weekend with no expectations. And she'd come out knowing it was possible to find a man she might love. Maybe Derek just wasn't that guy, but that didn't mean that their time together hadn't been the most wonderful experience of her life.

Tess groaned. "Or maybe he is the guy for me and I was too thick-headed to see it." Cursing softly, she reached for her phone and dialed Derek's number. It wasn't too late. She could get away this weekend. He'd bring the plane and they'd run away again and everything would go back to the way it was.

But he didn't answer his phone. And when the voicemail message began, she hung up, not sure what to say. It was better he didn't answer. She'd take some time to figure out what she was going to say before calling again.

Tess turned down the long drive to the farm, then smiled to herself. Her farm. It was the first piece of property that she or her father had ever owned. They'd been arguing for three weeks over a name and still hadn't decided on one. The rest of the neighbors still called it Halfpast Cottage Farm, though no one could explain the origin of the name.

As she neared the house, Tess saw a familiar car parked in the drive. She beeped the horn and as she pulled up, Alison got up from the porch steps and waved. Tess jumped out of the truck and ran up to her, giving her a fierce hug. "What are you doing here?"

"I had to come and see it," she said.

"You drove all this way?"

"I'm calling this a professional trip. I've got a meeting at Virginia Tech in Blacksburg this afternoon to talk about a research project. I thought I could spend the night with you and we could get some dinner later."

"You could stay with me," Tess said. "But I'm not sure you'd want to. Have you been inside the house?"

"No. Your dad offered to give me the tour, but I wanted to wait for you."

"I'll warn you in advance. We're going to have to find you a nice, cozy bed-and-breakfast for the night. We don't even have heat in this place. We've been keeping warm with space heaters in the bedrooms."

Alison slipped her arm around Tess's. "Show me. You forget, I grew up living on a school bus. I can handle just about anything."

They walked inside, stopping in the center hall and looking up the wide staircase. "You have to imagine it with fresh paint and furniture," Tess explained. "I want to furnish it with antiques, but not the pricey kind that adds character. You know, the shabby kind. I want it to be comfortable and cozy." She drew Alison along to the living room. "We have a fireplace. Although I'm afraid to start a fire in it for fear it needs a good cleaning first. And I can't afford a chimney sweep. But it looks nice."

Alison turned to face her. "So when are you going to mention Derek?" she asked. "The last time we spoke, you couldn't stop talking about him. And now it's like you're avoiding the subject."

"What do you expect?" Tess said. "Hi, Ali, so good to see you. By the way, I haven't heard from Derek this week and I'm worried."

"Really?"

Tess nodded. "He calls every Wednesday and asks if I'll spend the weekend with him. And every Wednesday, I've pushed him off. I just wanted to get settled first. Now, though, I think I'm ready to see him again but he hasn't called."

"Men get impatient," Alison said.

"But he told me he loved me. If he can't last for a few months, then I don't think he really loved me at all."

"Was this a test he was supposed to pass?"

Tess shook her head, then paused and shrugged. "I don't know. Maybe it was. Maybe I just wanted to see how hard he'd pursue me. I mean, when Jeffrey first came into my life, he never let up. He was at the farm every weekend."

"Don't compare Derek to Jeffrey," Alison warned. "That would be a huge mistake."

"You're right. Derek deserves better. He wasn't carrying on another relationship while we were together…I don't think."

Alison gave Tess's arm a squeeze. "I know how badly you were hurt by Jeffrey. But don't let that ruin what you and Derek have."

"Had?"

"No. If you're too scared to pursue this, then it will fall apart. A one-sided relationship will never work. But I think maybe this isn't one-sided. I think probably, deep inside, you know you're in love with him. And you just don't want to admit it yet."

Tess sighed. "I think about him all the time. At night, when I'm in bed, I close my eyes and I imagine he's with me. I can almost feel him there. But then, I realize it's just a fantasy."

"So call him. Invite him to visit for the weekend."

"Here?"

"Why not here? This is your home. And though it's a little rough right now, it's still yours."

"But he's used to so much nicer places. He lives in hotel suites with fancy bathrooms—and heat. I have a bed, a dresser and a mortgage. Oh, and mice. I have mice."

"But you've imagined him here, with you, haven't you?"

"I have. But there's always dinner cooking on the stove and a fire crackling in the fireplace and the two of us curled up together on the sofa. Unfortunately, I can't cook, the fireplace needs to be cleaned and I don't own a sofa. So, again, it's all just a very pretty fantasy."

"Do you love him? Yes or no?"

"I don't know," Tess said. "It's too soon."

"It's never too soon. I knew it the minute Drew stood beside me in my family's nativity scene, a silly head-dress on his head, wearing that awful purple shepherd's robe. We'd spent two nights together and it was perfectly clear to me that we were meant for each other."

"Love at first sight," Tess said.

"Not first sight. But pretty close to it. Listen to your heart, Tess. Trust your instincts."

"My instincts led me astray with Jeffrey," Tess said.

"No, they didn't, Tess. You didn't want to go to that party, even though you thought he was about to propose. And when Derek asked you to fly off with him, you didn't hesitate. Your instincts told you exactly what to do." Alison paused, then gathered Tess in her arms and gave her a hug. "I think you fell in love with Derek Nolan the moment you stepped on the elevator. Don't forget, I saw you in that hotel room before you took off into the night with a complete stranger. I saw how you looked at him. And how he looked at you. There was a spark there that neither one of you can deny."

Maybe she was in love with Derek. Madly and deeply and eternally in love with him. Who was to say she couldn't turn a wonderful fantasy into a real-life relationship. They'd been so good together on the island. And though life in the everyday world would have its ups and downs, Derek was exactly the kind of guy she wanted next to her when the "downs" happened.

Tess heard her father's voice echoing through the empty house. "Tessie! Tessie?"

"We're in the living room, Dad," she shouted.

He appeared in the doorway, his face flushed. His boots were dirty and he wore a pair of old leather gloves on his hands. "Did you get those hinges from the hardware store?"

"Hi, Mr. Robertson," Alison said.

"Hello there," he said, then turned back to Tess. "You got the right size, didn't you?"

"They're in the back of the truck. In the small bag."

He nodded. "I forgot to tell you. Our new neighbor stopped over this morning."

"Neighbor?"

"The guy who bought Ridgedale Farm. Name is Roland. He heard you might be interested in work and I said you'd stop by later this morning and talk to him. He doesn't seem like he knows a whit about horses. Probably just had a few million to play around with and decided horse farming might be fun." Her father shook his head and walked away. "What an idiot. He ought to thank his lucky stars you're livin' in the area so you can save his ass from disaster and…"

His voice faded as he walked back through the house. She glanced at Alison and smiled. "That's my dad."

"He seems like he's doing well."

"He still smokes too much. But since we bought this place, he hasn't been drinking. Probably part of that has to do with the fact he doesn't get a paycheck and he has no money of his own. But he's been working so hard all day that he just falls into bed at night. I think this was the best thing for him." Tess rubbed her arms. "Come on, let me show you the rest of the house and then I'll give you a tour of the barn."

DEREK WANDERED THROUGH the quiet house, taking time to look at all the details he'd missed the last time through. For a single guy, the house was huge—five bedrooms and four baths, spacious rooms with hardwood floors. Some of the furnishings had come along with the house—an added bonus—making the place seem more like a home from the moment he stepped in the front door.

His favorite room was already the library with its rich cherry paneling and floor-to-ceiling bookshelves. But he'd really bought the house for the porch. Like the house on Angel Cay, this one featured a wide verandah that circled both the first and second floor, offering beautiful views of the hilly countryside.

Ridgedale Farm was now officially his. He'd signed the papers the day before and picked up the keys that morning when he'd arrived at the airport. It had been the perfect solution to his problems with Tess. If she refused to come to him, then he was going to go to her. And what better excuse to keep her close than to ask her to run his horse farm for him.

Though there was every chance Tess wouldn't be interested, Derek had to believe she'd come around once she knew he was here to stay. Or he could have just made a three-million-dollar mistake. At least he now had a home, a bed that he could call his own.

Derek glanced at his watch. He'd hoped to see Tess earlier in the morning but when he'd arrived at her farm, she'd been off to town to fetch supplies. He'd met her father and chatted with him for a while, finding him a bit prickly and impatient.

He probably would have stuck around and waited a little longer for Tess, but George Robertson didn't seem interested in chatting. He did, however, express interest in the possibility of a job for his daughter at Ridgedale. Her dad had sold her outstanding managerial capabilities, and Derek had assured him that he'd be interested.

From what Derek could see of Tess's farm, she was in dire need of funds. The house was falling apart, the porch sagging and the windows peeling. It hadn't been painted for years and what was once white clapboard was now weathered gray wood. Even with her gambling winnings, the place had probably been all she could afford. But he had to admire her resolve. She was chasing her dream.

And now he was chasing his, Derek thought to himself. From the moment he stepped out of her pickup at the Lexington airport, Derek had struggled with his feelings. Common sense told him that three days wasn't enough to base the rest of his life on. But when he was away from Tess, he didn't feel complete.

She made him a better man. With her, he looked at things differently. He saw how fortunate he was and he'd come to appreciate everything he'd been given. Life wasn't all fancy hotels and private jets. Life was quiet moments on a beach or a perfect sunset, the kind of things that didn't cost a penny.

The sound of a car outside drew his attention and he pulled back the curtains. Tess's battered pickup pulled into the circular drive in front of the house. Standing back from the window, he watched as she got out.

She was just as beautiful as she'd always been. But this time, instead of a pretty evening gown or a sexy bikini, she was dressed in her everyday attire—faded jeans and riding boots. A canvas coat with a corduroy collar covered her T-shirt and she wore her hair pulled back in a ponytail, the thick waves falling over her collar.

A thrill shot through him and he found himself wondering how long he had to wait to kiss her. Could he pull her into his arms the moment he opened the door or should he wait and give her a chance to adjust to his presence there?

The doorbell rang. Running his hands through his hair, Derek strode to the foyer. He drew a deep breath and pulled the door open. When Tess saw him, her jaw dropped. Then she frowned and shook her head.

"What are you doing here?"

"Waiting for you," Derek said.

"How did you know I was coming?" She stopped short. "Did you come to the farm this morning and talk to my father?"

He nodded, his gaze dropping to her lips. He didn't want to talk—he wanted to act. It was taking every ounce of his willpower not to yank her into his arms and kiss her until she couldn't think straight. But Derek pulled the door open and stepped aside. "Come on in."

"You're Roland?"

"Who's Roland?"

"My father told me some guy named Roland came to see me this morning."

"Nolan," Derek said. "I told him my name was Nolan. He must have misunderstood."

"And you own this farm?"

He grinned. "Yep. I closed on it yesterday."

Tess stared at him as if he'd just sprouted horns and a tail. "You bought a horse farm?"

"No. I bought a farm. I don't have any horses so it's not technically a horse farm. But I have a lot of sheds and barns. So, there's plenty of room for horses…or chickens. Maybe some ducks. I like ducks."

"Oh my God," Tess said, pressing her fingers to her temples. "What have you done?"

"I don't know," Derek said. "What have I done?"

She strode across the room, then spun around to face him. "You spent millions on this property just so you could give me a job?"

"I spent millions so I could have a nice place to live… near you."

"Either way, you did this because of me. And if things don't work out, you're stuck with this place."

Derek held out his hands. "I like this place. It's quiet and I've got a lot of land." He walked over to her and grabbed her hand. "And I think you might like this place, too. Come on, I'll show you my favorite room in the house."

"I know your favorite room," she said, pulling away.

Frustrated, he grabbed her hand again. "No, you don't." Derek pulled her along to the library and pushed open the beveled-glass door. "This is my favorite room."

"There's a lot of empty shelves," she said.

"I know. But I figure we could spend a lifetime filling them up. You and me. Sitting here at night with a fire, reading. Just being together." He held up his hand. "I know what you're going to say. It's just a fantasy. But it isn't, Tess. It's a dream. There's a big difference between the two."

"We don't even know how we'd be off the island," she said.

"I think it's about time we find out. Here." Derek took her hand and brought it to his lips. "Let me show you more."

He pulled her along with him, out into the foyer and then onto the verandah. "I like this," he said. "A big porch is nice." They walked out into the yard and he pointed in the direction of the outbuildings. "Let me see if I can get this straight. According to my real estate agent, I have a stallion barn, a broodmare barn, two yearling barns, and a training barn. Plus, a manager's house, a dormitory for employees and the main house." He glanced up to gauge her reaction, but she was staring at him blankly. "And then there are lush pastures and quiet shaded lanes and fenced paddocks. And your own personal lake." He pointed off to the west. "It's over there."

This brought a smile from Tess. "You don't know anything about raising horses," she said. "You told me you'd never even ridden a horse."

He shrugged. "I'd have to hire someone who did know something about them. Someone really good. Not you, of course." He grinned at her. "Do you know anyone who might be looking for a job like that?"

"Let's say I do decide to manage this place for you. I've told you before, a horse farm is a horrible investment," she said, leaning up against the railing. "It's a money pit. Just buying breeding stock can cost millions. Good feed and vet care and training are more money on top of that. And you're not guaranteed a winner. The only way to make back your investment is by sheer luck. This is no business for dilettantes. It's a business for gamblers who have very, very deep pockets. Or for wealthy people who want to flaunt their wealth by wasting it on overpriced thoroughbreds."

"It's a wonder anyone ever hired you," Derek said. "You seem to have a very negative attitude about your chosen profession."

"If you don't really love it, and love the animals and the culture, then it will never be worth it."

"You love it," Derek said. "And I love you. So, I think I could really learn to love it. Tess, I want someplace to come home to and this seems like a good place. You'd be happy here, which is important to me."

Tess looked at him warily. "I just bought a farm."

"And I think you should live there…until you decide it's all right to live here."

"How do I know this will last? You could get bored with me, bored with horse breeding and decide to sell the farm."

"I'd never get bored with you," Derek said.

"That's not the point," Tess said.

"Then what is the point?"

"I—I don't want to make the same mistake twice."

Derek cursed softly. This was not going well. He'd expected some resistance, but she seemed to have a ready argument for every reason he gave. Fed up, Derek grabbed her waist and pulled her body against his. And then, as he'd done so many times before, he kissed her.

He began softly at first and then, as the kiss spun out, he grew more desperate, eager to prove that the passion was still alive between them. When she responded, he relaxed and invited her to take control. And when Tess wrapped her arms around his neck and sighed softly, Derek knew his life had just been made.

"You won't make the same mistake twice," he whispered. "You want to know why?"

Tess nodded, her gaze fixed on his.

"Because I love you. And I can't see my future with any woman but you. Every time I try to imagine it, you're there, Tess. Standing right next me."

"How is it possible this happened so fast?" Tess asked.

"I don't know. But if you feel better slowing down for a little while, I'm all right with that." He cupped her cheek in his hand. "Please, say you'll consider it."

"I can't," Tess said. A tiny smile twitched at the corners of her mouth. "Not until I've seen the bedroom."

With a low growl, Derek scooped her up into his arms and started toward the stairs. Tess screamed, holding on tight. "What are you doing?"

"What I've been thinking about doing for the past six weeks. I'm taking you to bed."

She didn't protest. Instead, she laughed all the way up the stairs. And when he tossed her on top of the comforter, Tess yanked him down on top of her. "All right," she murmured. "Let's see how this goes in the real world."

"I can guarantee you it's going to be even better," Derek said, tugging his jacket off and tossing it aside.

"Are we going to spend most of our time naked?"

Derek kissed the tip of her nose. "That point is entirely negotiable."

TESS ROLLED OVER, burying her face in the pillow to block out the late-afternoon light streaming through the windows. With a moan, she stretched, then curled back up against Derek's naked body.

She pressed her lips to his shoulder, inhaling the scent of his skin as she did. Nothing had changed. She'd tried her best to ignore what they had, but now that he was here, Tess couldn't delude herself any longer. She'd fallen hopelessly in love with Derek.

"I'm sorry," she whispered.

"For what," he said.

Tess hadn't realized he was awake. "You've been so patient with me. I've been flailing around trying to deal with all my emotional baggage." She drew a deep breath and let it out. "But I'm done now. I'm going to throw all the baggage in that lake you bought and I'm going to move forward."

"What does that mean, Tess?"

She reached out and grabbed his hand, then clutched it to her chest. "It means I think I'm in love with you. And I want to find out for sure. I want to crawl into bed with you at night and wake up in your arms. I want to live in this house with you. And I want to believe we have a future together."

"I've known we had a future together since the moment you walked into that elevator."

"How did you know?" Tess asked.

Derek slipped his arm around her waist and pulled her hips against his. He dropped a kiss on the top of her head. "I felt it. I knew you were something different, something special. You changed my whole world that night, Tess."

He bent lower and kissed her softly and Tess's pulse quickened. She loved how that happened, how every time he kissed her, her body seemed to melt into his. "Maybe we should go back to our nap."

"What nap? Were we sleeping?"

"You know what? I don't think our time on the island was a fantasy. I think it was real and we just didn't realize it until now. This is all real, all these feelings I have for you, all this excitement and anticipation. It's all real and it's the best thing that's ever happened to me. *You're* the best thing that's ever happened to me."

"I'm going to hold you to those words, Tess. Because in our life together, we'll probably hit some rough patches. But I want you to know, you're the woman I want to spend the rest of my days with…starting now."

"And starting in your bed?" she asked, laughing as he pulled her along.

"Our bed," Derek said. "Our house. And our life."

As they lost themselves in each other once again, Tess

was aware of every breath she took, every heartbeat in her body. Her future had finally found her, here with this man. And she'd found a home in his heart. Nothing could ever take that away from her.

* * * * *

HARLEQUIN® *Blaze*™

COMING NEXT MONTH

Available January 25, 2011

REQUEST YOUR FREE BOOKS!

2 FREE NOVELS
PLUS 2
FREE GIFTS!

HARLEQUIN®

Blaze™

Red-hot reads!

HB10R

*Harlequin Romance author Donna Alward is loved
for her gorgeous rancher heroes.*

*Meet Wyatt as he's confronted by both a precious
little pink bundle left on his doorstep and his neighbor Elli
who's going to show him the ropes....*

Introducing
PROUD RANCHER, PRECIOUS BUNDLE

THE SQUAWKING QUIETED as Elli picked the baby up, and Wyatt turned around, trying hard to ignore the feelings of inadequacy as Darcy immediately stopped fussing.

"Maybe she's uncomfortable. What do you think, sweetheart?" Elli turned her conversation to the baby.

"What do you think is wrong?" Wyatt asked, putting the coffee pot back on the burner.

A strange look passed over Elli's face, one that looked like guilt and panic. But it was gone quickly. "I couldn't say," she replied.

"But you were so good with her this afternoon." Wyatt put his hands on his hips.

"Lucky, that's all. I just…remembered a few things." The same strange look flitted over her features once more.

Wyatt took the coffee to the table. "You fooled me. You looked like you knew exactly what you were doing." So much so that Wyatt had felt completely inept. A feeling he despised. He was used to being the one in control.

Elli and Darcy walked the length of the kitchen and back. After a few moments, she admitted, "I haven't really cared for a baby before. The things I thought of were simply things I'd heard about. Not from experience, Mr. Black."

Her chin jutted up, closing the subject but making him

want to ask the questions now pulsing through his mind. But then he remembered the old saying—*Don't look a gift horse in the mouth*. He'd benefit from whatever insight she had and be glad of it.

"I don't really know what babies need," he said. "I fed her, patted her back like you did, walked her to sleep, but every time I put her down…"

Wyatt almost groaned. Of course. He'd forgotten one important thing. He'd been so focused on getting the formula the right temperature that he'd forgotten to check her diaper. Not that he had any clue what to do there either.

Pulling calves and shoveling out stalls was far less intimidating than one tiny newborn.

"She's probably due for a diaper change, isn't she." He tried to sound nonchalant. This was a perfect opportunity. Elli must know how to change a diaper. He could simply watch her so he'd know better for the next time.

Instead, Elli came around the corner of the counter and placed Darcy back in his arms. "Here you go, Uncle Wyatt," she said lightly. "You get diaper duty. I'll fix the coffee. Cream and sugar?"

Oh boy, Wyatt thought, looking down into Darcy's pursed face, his smug plan blown to smithereens. He was in for it now.

Will sparks fly between Elli and Wyatt?

Find out in
PROUD RANCHER, PRECIOUS BUNDLE
Available February 2011 from Harlequin Romance

Try these Healthy and Delicious Spring Rolls!

INGREDIENTS

2 packages rice-paper spring roll wrappers (20 wrappers)

1 cup grated carrot

¼ cup bean sprouts

1 cucumber, julienned

1 red bell pepper, without stem and seeds, julienned

4 green onions finely chopped— use only the green part

DIRECTIONS

1. Soak one rice-paper wrapper in a large bowl of hot water until softened.

2. Place a pinch each of carrots, sprouts, cucumber, bell pepper and green onion on the wrapper toward the bottom third of the rice paper.

3. Fold ends in and roll tightly to enclose filling.

4. Repeat with remaining wrappers. Chill before serving.

Find this and many more delectable recipes including the perfect dipping sauce in

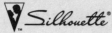

ROMANTIC
S U S P E N S E
Sparked by Danger, Fueled by Passion.

NEW YORK TIMES BESTSELLING AUTHOR
RACHEL LEE
No Ordinary Hero

Strange noises...a woman's mysterious disappearance
and a killer on the loose who's too close for comfort.

With no where else to turn, Delia Carmody looks
to her aloof neighbour to help, only to discover
that Mike Windwalker is no ordinary hero.

Conard County THE NEXT GENERATION

Available in December.
Wherever books are sold.

Visit Silhouette Books at www.eHarlequin.com

SRS27709R

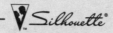

SPECIAL EDITION

FROM *USA TODAY* BESTSELLING AUTHOR

CHRISTINE RIMMER

COMES AN ALL-NEW BRAVO FAMILY TIES STORY.

Donovan McRae has experienced
the greatest loss a man can face, and
while he can't forgive himself, life—
and Abilene Bravo's love—are still
waiting for him. Can he find it in himself
to reach out and claim them?

Look for

DONOVAN'S CHILD

available February 2011

HARLEQUIN *Presents*

USA TODAY bestselling author

Sharon Kendrick

introduces

HIS MAJESTY'S CHILD

The king's baby of shame!

King Casimiro harbors a secret—no one in the kingdom
of Zaffirinthos knows that a devastating accident has left
his memory clouded in darkness. And Casimiro himself
cannot answer why Melissa Maguire, an enigmatic English
rose, stirs such feelings in him…. Questioning his ability
to rule, Casimiro decides he will renounce the throne.
But Melissa has news she knows will rock the palace
to its core—*Casimiro has an heir!*

Law dictates Casimiro cannot abdicate, so he must find a
way to reacquaint himself with Melissa—his new queen!

**Available from Harlequin Presents
February 2011**

www.eHarlequin.com

HP12972